He looked as if he had never seen her previously

But then she'd never been like this previously. Beautiful, charming, witty—and growing more confident by the minute.

She moved closer to Alex, aware that the increasing number of dancers was giving her the perfect excuse to close the gap between them. "Gina . . . ." She felt the tension in him as his arms tightened around her, their bodies moving in precise harmony to the music, to each other.

With a gentle natural movement she leaned her cheek against his shoulder, her breasts pressing against the hardness of his chest, not stopping to think that she might be playing with fire.

Not once did it occur to her that she might lose control, that when she had finally got Alex Craig where she wanted him, her little game could backfire . . . .

WELCOME
TO THE WONDERFUL WORLD
OF *Harlequin Romances*

Interesting, informative and entertaining,
each Harlequin Romance portrays an appealing
and original love story. With a varied array
of settings, we may lure you on an African safari,
to a quaint Welsh village, or an exotic Riviera
location—anywhere and everywhere that adventurous
men and women fall in love.

As publishers of Harlequin Romances, we're
extremely proud of our books. Since 1949,
Harlequin Enterprises has built its publishing
reputation on the solid base of quality and
originality. Our stories are the most popular
paperback romances sold in North America; every
month, six new titles are released and sold at
nearly every book-selling store in Canada and the
United States.

A free catalogue listing all Harlequin Romances
can be yours by writing to the

HARLEQUIN READER SERVICE,
(In the U.S.) 1440 South Priest Drive, Tempe, AZ 85281
(In Canada) Stratford, Ontario N5A 6W2

We sincerely hope you enjoy reading
this Harlequin Romance.

Yours truly,

THE PUBLISHERS
  Harlequin Romances

Lesson in Love

by

CLAUDIA JAMESON

Harlequin Books

TORONTO • NEW YORK • LOS ANGELES • LONDON
AMSTERDAM • PARIS • SYDNEY • HAMBURG
STOCKHOLM • ATHENS • TOKYO • MILAN

Original hardcover edition published in 1982
by Mills & Boon Limited

ISBN 0-373-02523-8

Harlequin Romance first edition January 1983

*With many thanks to Rica and Tony . . .
two of Africa's brightest diamonds.*

CHAPTER ONE

GINA realised that the journey from London to Kenya must be tiring at the best of times, but she was in no way prepared for a fourteen-hour nightmare in getting to her destination. Travelling from London to Nairobi all through the night had been boring and uncomfortable. The massive jumbo jet had been filled to capacity, so there were no empty seats to curl up on; the man on her left had drunk whisky throughout the night and stank of it, the woman on her right had been at least eight stones overweight and snored loudly, incessantly.

Trapped between her unpleasant fellow passengers, in that strange half-light which prevails on aeroplanes flying through the night, sleep had become impossible for Gina . . . as it had so often of late.

The blazing spectacle of the sunrise over Africa, a sight which might have held her enthralled at any other time, had held not the slightest excitement for her today. She wished it had not been necessary to leave London. Her neck was stiff from having her head propped up on one hand for so long and she had an ache in her lower back because she'd been obliged to sit down in a confined space for hours.

Even the rustic colours of the earth, the rich redness of the soil where the composition of the land changed, the glimpses of Nairobi's massive National Safari Park, had failed to put her in the mood for a holiday in Africa. But then this wasn't really a holiday. Gina was making the five-thousand-mile journey especially to see her father. Nothing else would have enticed her to Africa.

It might not have been so bad if the journey had ended in Nairobi, if her father had chosen to live there where it was probably quite civilised, instead of in some Godforsaken town where the electricity failed as often as it worked, where the water was in short supply and the nearest neighbours for two miles were the snakes that inhabited the bush. Such was the information about Malindi, the place where her father had settled, gleaned from the recent letter from him. Never in a million years would Gina understand why a wealthy man like her father had chosen to retire to some thoroughly uncivilised spot on the African continent. That her equally wealthy, ever-immaculate new American stepmother had agreed to live there would forever remain an even greater mystery to Gina.

The plane she was now on was taking her down to Malindi. On the coast. Where the mosquitos flourished. And if she'd thought the first part of her journey was uncomfortable, it was nothing to what she was going through now. She was on board an old fifty-seater aeroplane that looked as if it were held together by chewing gum, that was bumping and lurching, dropping dozens of feet at a time as it hit air pocket after air pocket. When boarding this plane Gina had made a beeline for a window seat. Only now was she realising her mistake. As if it weren't bad enough that the interior of the plane was like a hot dry oven, the scorching glare of a relentless sun was almost burning one side of her face despite the little curtain she'd drawn across the oval window.

A slow throbbing started in her temples, like the rhythmic beat of a jungle drum. A feeling of nausea invaded her stomach, threatening imminent embarrassment with every twist and turn of the aircraft. It was frightening, really frightening. Only the thought of her father stopped her from bursting into tears.

She missed her father acutely. She never had seen enough of him; all her life she had been obliged to travel if she wanted to spend some time with him—although never before to Africa. And then she had had his company only in brief snatches, during the holidays from boarding school, and often not even then if he'd been conducting business abroad. 'When you're older,' he used to say, 'when you leave school, we'll have a long, long holiday together. We'll take twelve months and travel round the world!'

But the promise was never fulfilled. When Gina finally left boarding school, Harry Duncan then insisted she go on to finishing school. 'I want you to have the advantages I never had,' he had insisted. And so she was packed off to Switzerland for a year. And she'd hated it. Just as she'd hated boarding school—the regimentation, the discipline, the nights in impersonal dormitories which were never quite warm enough in the winters and stifling in the summers. Then there were the weekends. Weekends which most of the girls looked forward to. A weekend with their families. Gina was always one of the minority who had to remain at school because their families were too far away—or otherwise engaged. With Gina's father it was both. Business always came first. But she held no resentment. Her father had done his best, had given her a good and expensive education. And everything she wanted . . . materially.

She sighed, pulling her safety belt a little tighter, one hand reaching up to make small, circular movements against the side of her temple in a futile effort to ease the increasing throbbing. Her mouth was dry, her lips and tongue absolutely parched, although her body was soaked in perspiration. She felt an absolute wreck. At the best of times, she never bothered dressing up—didn't bother much about her appearance at all. But she felt so stupid now, dressed in faded denims and a white woollen sweater that had been so appropriate for the chilly March winds in London. It had even been appropriate for the temperature in the other plane. But it had been night-time then. Many miles ago.

The African sun at its meridian makes a fierce enemy against the uninitiated. She must treat it with respect when she reached her destination. *When* she reached it—the thought made her nervous. How was she going to hide from her father the fact that she disliked his new wife? How was she going to cope with the bitchy Stella when she was to spend three whole weeks in her company? What was it about that woman that made Gina distrust her? Worse, what was her father going to say when she told him she'd dropped out of art school?

Art school! She hadn't wanted to go there in the first place. For Gina it had been yet another institution. But her father had seized upon her talent for art—her only talent—and insisted she develop it. Again he had insisted. Again their world trip had been postponed while Gina was installed in art school and her father went on working, working.

If only her mother had survived it might have been so different. But she had died giving birth to Gina, and all her young life, during those emotionally cold, institutionalised years when she had been starved for the warmth and constancy of family love Gina had wondered whether her father blamed her for his wife's death, had put her out of his life deliberately.

But she no longer thought in those terms. Her father did not hold, and never had held, any kind of resentment. He loved her as much as she loved him—and that was a lot. No, Harry Duncan had been a workaholic. He had been driven by something—not his wife's death, because he was a rich man even before that occurred—but something . . . well, who could explain it? Whatever it was, it had driven Harry on and on over a thirty-year span from being the manager of a single grocer's shop to being the owner of a vast chain of supermarkets which had made Duncan almost a household name in Britain. Gina was proud of him, very proud. And no, she'd have seen little more of him even if her mother had survived to make them into a real family.

And of course it was nice to have money; Gina knew that as well as her father. Not that she had any of her own; the money her mother had left her was in trust, not to be touched until she reached the age of twenty-five—

that was six years hence. But Gina didn't care about that; she had a generous allowance from her father in the meantime. Besides, unlike him she did not consider money to be the be-all and end-all in life. All she wanted from life was to be happy. Happiness was something that had eluded her for a long time, and she knew from experience that it couldn't be bought.

What use was money when she couldn't sleep at night? When lately she had experienced a growing discontent it was very hard to pinpoint, a feeling of something . . . something missing . . . something approaching panic . . . a nervousness she knew to be unfounded but was helpless to prevent? She had undergone some sort of change lately, she realised that much, and deep inside herself she knew it was not a change for the better. She had become very tense, nervy—a condition which was not helping her through this harrowing flight.

But then all this was part of Gina's reasons for travelling to see her father. If he'd been on the moon she'd have got there somehow. There had been many times when she had missed him in the past, times when he was not available. But he was available now. He had retired from business and Gina knew exactly where to find him. And at this particular time in her life she wasn't merely missing him, she needed him. Really *needed* him. Not only was he her only parent, he was the shrewdest, most positive person she knew. He would help her. He would know *how* to help her. She was yearning to have a long, long talk with him; to explain her reasons for dropping out of art school and to tell him of her plans—tentative plans—for the future . . . if she could just get him away from his possessive wife for a few hours.

Part of Gina's dislike of her elegant, sophisticated new stepmother was that she had completely monopolised Harry, had even enticed him away from his own country, for if they hadn't chosen to settle in some obscure little African town then they would have ended up living in

Stella's reportedly palatial house in Boston, Massachusetts.

During the few days Gina had so far spent in Stella's company, when Harry had introduced her as a 'special friend', the older woman had made it plain that she wouldn't consider living in England even though, as she had hastened to add, 'It is a lovely country and I do like to come here now and then to pick up a few things from your famous department store in Knightsbridge.' She'd said it in the most charming way possible, but it was something else which didn't go down well with Gina.

Shortly after that encounter Harry had accompanied Stella back to America—and married her there. That had hapepened eight months ago. Gina began her second year at art school, and kissed goodbye for ever to the promised world trip.

It not only irritated but also amazed Gina that her father had chosen Stella, of all people, to settle down with. Almost twenty years his junior, twice divorced and totally unsuitable for him, Stella Portman was sophisticated to the point of being glamorous, while Harry was staid, even Victorian in many ways. As far as Gina was concerned the pair of them were as different as chalk and cheese.

A rich woman in her own right, at least Stella couldn't be accused of gold-digging, although the way she had acquired her wealth, by way of two fat settlements from ex-husbands, was something else which didn't say much for her character. Furthermore, at nineteen Gina was convinced that anyone who had been through two divorces must be hopeless at building relationships. For her father's sake she hoped it would be a case of third time lucky, because from all accounts Harry seemed to adore his new wife . . .

'Oh, oh, help me! Please help me!' The clipped, frantic voice of the high-caste Indian woman sitting across the aisle snapped Gina out of her thoughts. She had noticed the woman as they boarded, very beautifully dressed in a white sari and carrying a tiny baby who looked no more than one month old. As she saw the woman sway forward in her seat at an instant when the plane was fairly level, Gina realised she was about to drop the child she had been cradling so protectively in her arms.

Without a thought of buzzing for the stewardesses, who were strapped into their seats like everybody else, Gina released the lock on her safety belt and staggered towards the Indian woman, trying desperately to offset the movement of the plane by pushing her back against the outer aisle seat as she reached for the baby.

The woman's head went down just as her hands reached towards the seat in front of her. Gina thought she had fainted—but no. Before she had been able to pull out the regulation brown bag from the pocket of the other seat, the woman vomited. And vomited.

Watching helplessly as the poor woman went into a spasm of retching, Gina bent her knees and deliberately slithered towards the floor, her back still pressing hard for balance against the metal support of the seat. Her own activity had caused the throbbing in her head to reach an unbearable pitch and she clung tightly to the baby, realising they would both be safer on the floor. She knew she was in danger of passing out as the pungent smell from across the aisle reached her nostrils, intensified by the stifling heat, and the plane started to shift around before her eyes in a way that had nothing to do with the turbulence outside.

Everything happened so quickly. There was a bottle of smelling salts under her nose, two pairs of legs before her eyes, a buzzing in her ears. And just an instant when she'd blacked out—before or after the baby had been taken from her, she didn't know.

With the aid of one stewardess Gina slumped into the aisle seat with her temples pounding so frantically she felt sure her head would explode. The other stewardess clung tightly to the Indian baby until someone volunteered to take it from her so that the mother might be helped.

Then the first girl was apologising profusely to Gina for something completely beyond her control. 'Madam, I'm so sorry. We're having a particularly bad run . . . haven't been able to bring round any refreshments . . . no water, I'm afraid, something's gone wrong with the mechanism . . . not surprising.'

Gina wiped the back of her hand across her forehead as beads of cold perspiration trickled down her face, on to her eyelashes, down the side of her nose. She could hardly hear, her ears were buzzing so loudly as an effect of the pressure inside the small cabin and the throbbing in her head.

'. . . Can you bring me anything? Please, something, anything to drink?' She dropped her head down between her knees and used every ounce of willpower to prevent the faint which was still threatening.

The next thing she knew was a glass of orange juice being thrust into her hand and the warning of a female voice. 'Don't drink it quickly, madam, it's ice cold.' Somewhere beyond that voice was another, hollow-sounding voice saying something about beginning a descent in a few minutes, and would the stewardesses please return to their seats.

But the girl who had brought the drink never got the chance. As if in direct defiance of the Captain, the little plane chose that moment to lurch forwards and downwards so violently that the stewardess was flung face-down on to the aisle. In those split seconds, as if in slow motion, Gina saw the orange juice rise vertically from her glass to hang momentarily in mid-air before it splattered all over the front of her sweater. There was the sudden ice-cold shock against the heat of her body as the liquid instantly soaked through the wool, and the horrid feeling that her stomach had risen up into her throat. She heard the involuntary cries of the other passengers as handbags, pens, newspapers, hats and spectacles scattered all over the floor.

At the instant when the plane came to an absolute

standstill there was an unnatural, hushed silence—and then a joint sigh of relief from everyone on board. The landing had been astonishingly smooth, in fact the plane had levelled off completely after the descent had begun, but it seemed that until they had come to a standstill nobody had been taking anything for granted.

Gina took a moment to say a silent thank-you and to try to steady her nerves before she attempted to move. Her dark hair was soaked in perspiration, the wispy fringe plastered against her forehead. Her feet had swollen so much from the heat that she could hardly get her shoes back on. She knew her back was bruised because every movement she made was hurting her.

The Indian woman smiled over at her weakly and Gina smiled weakly back. Her nerves were shot, her hands trembling as she hitched her canvas shoulder-bag into place and picked up her hand luggage. She looked down helplessly at her stained sweater. What sort of bitchy remark would Stella make about that? As she moved towards the exit Gina shrugged philosophically; her father was here, now, just a few minutes' walk away, so everything was worthwhile—the nightmare journey, the pain in her back, the swollen feet, everything. Even the tensions which were gripping her this very moment—and that inexplicable nervousness which had been consuming her on and off for the past few months.

The airport itself was more like an overgrown tin hut. Really, it was just as she thought. This place, this—Malindi—was in the back of beyond. As she walked tiredly along the tarmac under the scorching glare of a relentless sun, Gina turned around to take a final look at the plane which had just about managed to get her here. She saw that she was one of only five people who had disembarked. The rest of the passengers were obviously flying on to Mombasa, and she pitied them as much as they must surely be dreading it.

Several Kenyans were attending to the retrieval of suitcases from the plane's luggage hold, and Gina found some small consolation in realising she wouldn't have long to wait for her baggage.

The shelter of the airport building was a blessed relief. Before her eyes had had time to adjust to the relative darkness, Gina was looking for her father. There was no sign of him. In fact there was nobody there at all. Nobody to meet the other passengers. Just one huge black man smiling broadly to himself as he slowly pushed a sweeping brush back and forth.

When her large suitcase was dumped at her feet by another broadly smiling African, Gina sat down on it and waited. And waited. She felt very close to tears. How inconsiderate of them to be late! Tense, sick, nervous and thoroughly exhausted from lack of sleep, she watched her few fellow passengers walking out of the building, at an exit just a few yards away. She got to her feet and dragged her suitcase towards it. From there, at least she could watch for her father's car.

Just as she got there, a tall, strikingly handsome man strode past her. Gina's head turned involuntarily to get a better look at him. Over six feet tall, the man moved lithely, purposefully. With a mild sense of shock that a white man would do such a thing, Gina saw that he was wearing nothing more than a plain white piece of cloth, knee-length and tied at the waist. Apart from that, and a pair of leather sandals, he was naked. Apparently! He was also golden, from the top of his yellow-blond hair to the tip of his sandal-clad feet. A remarkably handsome man, she acknowledged, her eyes travelling over the broad, muscular expanse of his deeply tanned back as he continued to walk through the building. When he stopped and turned, Gina whipped her head around, not wanting to be caught looking. A man such as he was no doubt used to turning the heads of the opposite sex.

The car park didn't need much scanning. There was no sign of her father, or even Stella. In fact the only vehicle now to be seen was a tatty old Land Rover, so old and battered that large chunks of rust were clearly visible even at a distance.

Having just perched herself once more on her suitcase, Gina was startled by a sudden tap on the shoulder. Her head moved round, then upwards, until she found herself eye to eye with the Adonis who had passed by her a couple of minutes earlier.

'Miss Duncan? Georgina Duncan?' The rich, mellow tones of his ruggedly masculine voice were vaguely disconcerting, as was his stance, the proximity of him as he towered over her, and a certain arrogance in the way he held his head.

'Y—Yes?'

'I'm Alex Craig,' he began, as he appraised her slowly from head to foot, disapproval of what he saw unmistakable in his eyes. 'I've come to collect you. I'm a friend of your father and I'm Stella's——'

'Collect me? But why?' The questions burst from her. Couldn't her father be bothered to collect her personally? After she'd come five thousand miles to see him? She was instantly upset. Didn't her father want her here?

'Where is my father?' she demanded then. 'What's he doing that he can't be bothered to drive here himself? And where is *she*—Stella?'

Alex Craig's eyes narrowed thoughtfully at her tone of voice, but Gina hardly noticed. 'I have bad news for you,' he said quietly, 'Stella and Harry have gone away——'

'Gone away?' Again Gina's voice came out in a thoughtless burst born of a crushing, immeasurable sense of disappointment. She could hardly believe this was happening, that yet again her father wasn't here when she needed him. That he'd gone away when he knew full well she was coming to stay with him. As these thoughts flashed through her mind within split seconds, her devastating disappointment turned into anger and she thrashed out unthinkingly.

'Well, that's bloody charming! No, don't tell me, I can

guess! Stella wanted some new clothes, so she's persuaded my father to pop over to Paris for the weekend!'

'You're one hell of a rude young woman!' The deep voice bellowed so loudly, so unexpectedly that Gina nearly fell off her suitcase. She was stunned, momentarily confused as disappointment and anger at her father continued to consume her. All that, plus the realisation that she had, indeed, sounded rude.

'I'm sorry, Mr Craig. Forgive me, I know all this has nothing to do with you, but I've had such a bad flight and I'm——'

'That's the luck of the draw!' he informed her harshly, bellowing so loudly that the throbbing in Gina's head started up again. 'I accept no excuses for that sort of rudeness. I don't care for your attitude, and I don't care to be constantly cut off in mid-sentence.'

'But——'

'Shut up and listen!' he said, doing to her precisely what she'd done to him—but far more aggressively.

Unsure whether it was his total, unreasonable rejection of her sincere apology, the sheer volume of his voice, or just the enormous strength of the man which silenced her, Gina fell silent.

Alex Craig's head lifted very slightly. It was a gesture of superiority, satisfaction. 'Now then, I would have told you this more gently, but since you are obviously totally insensitive, I'll give it to you straight . . .'

As he spoke, now at normal pitch, he stepped closer to her so that Gina became aware only of his eyes. Beautifully set off by long blond lashes, they were the bluest eyes she'd ever seen. Deep, deep blue. There were laughter lines at the corners of them, tiny crinkles where the skin was slightly paler against the depth of his tan. This was a man who obviously spent most of his time in the sun, and a good deal of his time laughing—probably at the world in general. But there was no humour visible in his eyes now, there was nothing but an open animosity she didn't deserve.

As he said his piece, Gina's eyes moved away from his to travel almost unseeingly over the generous, sensuous mouth, the firm jawline and square chin, until she was looking nowhere in particular. His news was upsetting.

'. . . It's your Uncle Ralph. He's had a heart attack, and your father's gone to Australia to see him. Naturally, Stella has gone with him. . . . Georgina, do you hear me?'

She heard him all right. It was indeed bad news. She could just imagine how her father was feeling . . . Uncle Ralph had emigrated over twenty years ago and Harry had seen his brother only twice during those years, and each time had been when Ralph had made the visit to England. Harry would be feeling guilty. Quite apart from that he would be alarmed, because he himself had a heart condition—angina. Oh, he'd assured Gina it was nothing serious, but it was shortly after the diagnosis last year that Harry had retired from business.

'Yes, I hear you.' Gina's eyes travelled back to the face of the man who had been sent to give her a lift, and again she fell silent.

She was upset for Uncle Ralph, even though she hardly knew him. She was upset for his wife. Most of all she was concerned for her father. He had obviously had no choice but to go and see his brother. It wasn't Harry's fault that he couldn't be here. Not this time. He was probably just as disappointed as she was.

But Alex Craig had no idea what had just gone through her mind, so it was that Gina's next remark—an unfortunate one—angered him even further. She muttered it almost to herself, just the tail end of a thought as she realised her predicament and acknowledged that she felt a little afraid, being in a strange country where she didn't know a soul. 'I wish they'd let me know. They could have spared me that journey——'

'My God!' he exploded. 'Is that all you have to say after what I've just told you? Is that all you can think about—yourself? First you have a tantrum, now you're behaving like a spoiled brat!'

All the tiredness, all the anxieties and tensions of the past fourteen hours suddenly came to a head and made something inside Gina snap. Rather than feeling upset at being misunderstood, she got angry. From his lofty plane this Alex Craig person thought he'd summed her up in the space of a few minutes. And he'd tried and sentenced her to boot! Spoiled brat, indeed! How could he say that, when he had no idea what she was thinking, how she was feeling? She had apologised for her original outburst, and he had responded by lashing into her. Well, she wasn't going to apologise again, not when her remark had been an innocent one and he had retaliated so viciously.

She hadn't deserved that insult—and she wasn't going to let him get away with it! She leapt to her feet to face the man from her full height—five feet four in flat shoes— and defended herself with justifiable indignation.

'Mr Craig, you looked at me as if I were something despicable before we even spoke to one another. I'm aware of how I look, and I'm not exactly proud of it. I'm also aware of how I sounded at first, and I apologised for it. But I resent your last remark—and I'll thank you not to pass judgment when you're not in command of all the facts, when you've no idea *why* I look like this, when you've no idea what I'm thinking, and even less of what I'm feeling!'

'Feeling?' he scoffed. 'When your first consideration was the inconvenience you'd been put to? My dear Georgina, you were clearly the last in the queue when God handed out feelings! Those—among other things.'

Well, that was plain enough for anyone! Alex Craig had obviously taken an instant dislike to her and was not going to change his mind. She tried to tell herself it didn't matter at all . . . but she was upset. She didn't like being misjudged. Furthermore, he was wrong—so very wrong! She did consider other people's feelings. She was not insensitive. In fact, she was too sensitive for her own good at times—like now, as she wondered what he'd meant by his last remark.

But Gina Duncan was very adept at hiding her feelings when necessary. It came with years of practice. Only those people whom she could really trust, like Charles and her two flatmates, Dinah and Sue, ever came remotely close to knowing what was really in her heart. And not even to them did she tell everything.

The tears, the disappointment and frustration she wanted to give vent to now were kept well under control. 'All right, Mr Craig, enough is enough.' Her voice was hard. 'You came here to give me a lift. Shall we go?'

'Why, Georgina, that's the first sensible thing you've said since you arrived!'

His sarcasm made her sigh inwardly. If only he knew how her head was throbbing, her feet were hurting, her back ... but would it have made any difference? No, there was only one way to treat the likes of him. Whoever he was. She would treat him from now on in the way he treated her. For the duration of this journey—however long it might be—she would give as good as she got.

She looked up at him levelly, fixing him with a dark, Scorpionic gaze from eyes that revealed no emotion whatsoever.

'Don't call me Georgina,' she said coldly. 'Nobody but my father calls me that. The name's Gina—but you may call me Miss Duncan.'

For an instant she thought she saw the corners of his mouth twitch. 'I see,' he said, his voice ridiculously sugar-sweet. 'Well, if Miss Duncan would care to step aside, her humble chauffeur will pick up her suitcase and drive her home!'

'I can manage my own suitcase, thank you.'

'Pick the bloody thing up, then,' he snapped suddenly, as the fleeting humour that had appeared in his eyes vanished instantly. 'I've got better things to do than stand around airports talking to ill-mannered schoolgirls.'

She was not at all surprised that he actually let her carry her own suitcase. Oh, but she paid dearly for that stubborn, independent streak in her! As soon as she lifted it she almost dropped it again. The pain in her back almost creased her. But she was damned if she'd let it show.

Alex Craig strode out of the building in a similar way to that in which he had entered it, with lithe, panther-like strides, easily, purposefully—but quite slowly. This whole place had an air of slowness about it, as if it didn't belong to the real world. Probably nobody did anything in a hurry here; it was far too hot for haste.

Within seconds of being under the blazing sun Gina realised the accuracy of her thoughts. Beads of perspiration were trickling down her back, between her breasts, beneath the waistband of her well-worn jeans. She paused, switching the weighty suitcase from one hand to the other as she looked around for Mr Craig's car. Where on earth had he parked it?

When she saw him come to a halt at the side of the rickety old Land Rover, then lean against it as he watched her struggling with her case, her hand-luggage and shoulder bag, she cringed.

'Surely you haven't come to collect me in *that*!' she blurted as she finally caught up with him and panted for breath. Wasn't her nightmare over yet? Was this, the third lap of her journey, going to be as bad as the previous two? She was cringing at the thought of how her back would be feeling after a ride in this uncomfortable-looking vehicle on roads she just knew would not be smooth ones. Not in this part of the country.

Needless to say, she'd made quite the wrong comment as far as Alex Craig was concerned. 'So you're a snob as well as an inconsiderate spoiled brat?'

'Snobbery has nothing to do with it!' she snapped. Her glance registered that one of the Land Rover's hub-caps was missing, one of the mudguards was missing, the cloth which was supposed to cover the framework on the open back section was hanging in tatters and the tyres would be regarded as illegal in England.

'That vehicle wouldn't be allowed on the roads in England. It doesn't look safe, and it's a filthy disgrace!'

Alex Craig appraised her slowly, his eyes travelling upwards from her now dusty shoes to her crumpled denims to her once white sweater plastered with orange juice, now stiffened and dried into the wool. He grunted, disgusted. 'Quite so. It's eminently suitable for its passenger.' And with that he heaved her suitcase into the back of the truck as if it were a feather, then walked away from her, making no attempt to help her into the passenger seat.

Of course, the passenger seat had a split in the upholstery and the ashtrays were overflowing. On the floor there was a scattering of dirt, old dried mud, and from the driving mirror hung a gaudy furry ape whose head began to nod as Alex Craig heaved himself into the driver's seat.

With a sideways look at him as he thrust the gear-lever into first and did a far-too-rapid U-turn, Gina found herself consumed with curiosity about the man who had come to collect her. Who was Alex Craig? What was he? What was he in connection with her father, a wealthy man who usually mixed with other wealthy men? Was he some sort of employee, perhaps? No, Harry Duncan's employees would not be seen driving a vehicle such as this. Some sort of eccentric, then? Whatever—eccentric or not—this couldn't possibly be his car. It just didn't fit. He was too . . . too proud . . . to own a vehicle such as this. There was something aristocratic about his profile, a certain pride in the way he held himself, the way he walked. Arrogance was nearer the word! And a heap too much self-confidence.

He drove quickly, assuredly, along roads which would be considered dirt tracks in England. It was a bumpy ride—and painful. For a long time nothing was said. Alex Craig had obviously lost all inclination for conversation—

such as it would be between them. Gina was concentrating on trying to keep completely upright and still, to ignore the ache in her lower back and the pain where she'd hurt it higher up. She was also thinking about her father and saying a silent prayer for his brother.

'How bad is it with Uncle Ralph?' she asked at length. 'I mean, it must be very serious if Daddy's gone . . .' Her voice trailed away.

'So you're interested after all?' She was prepared for further sarcasm and he didn't disappoint her. 'I was wondering how long it would be before you got around to asking. Or do you have an ulterior motive in asking that question, for instance all you really want to know is when your father will be back?'

'I'm just asking what happened with my uncle—all right?'

He took his eyes off the road and fixed them on her for a dangerously long time—as if she were undergoing yet another appraisal. 'All right. It seems that your uncle's attack is a massive one. It's really touch and go, I'm sorry to say. And unfortunately it took three hours before his wife could get a call through to your father. I'm afraid the coastal telephones here are not the most reliable instruments.'

'I'm surprised to hear they have them at all,' said Gina, with genuine surprise. Her father hadn't mentioned a telephone number in his letter, which had given merely a Malindi P.O. box as an address. It surprised her there was any sort of telephone system. From what she could see from the windows of the Land Rover—miles and miles of nothingness—this place appeared to be nothing but a hot and dusty hellhole without one redeeming feature.

'The upshot is,' said Alex Craig, his voice clipped as if she had annoyed him again in some way, 'that your father and Stella took off from Malindi airport precisely three hours ago. By now they'll be on a flight from Nairobi to Sydney, probably with a couple of changes en route.'

'And you've no idea when he'll be back.'

'And I've no idea when he'll be back. It'll depend on Ralph's condition, of course.'

Gina sighed, putting both hands flat on the seat in an effort to take some pressure off her back. 'So I've passed him virtually in mid-air?'

'Yep,' he said shortly. Then, 'You realise now that they had no chance of letting you know. You must have left London—what—about fourteen hours ago? Possibly more.'

Gina nodded. It was just one of those things; nobody's fault, nothing anyone could do. No time for postponement. She was just about to ask whether her father had left any sort of message—anything at all—when he pre-empted her.

'Stella sends her apologies. She was really very upset about it all.'

Stella sends her apologies? Precisely what was she upset about?

By sheer coincidence, Alex Craig answered that thought, too. 'She was upset for Harry, naturally. But she was very concerned about you.'

Oh, really! Stella must be quite an actress if she'd managed to give that impression! 'But of course she was! She must have been absolutely devastated to miss me!'

Gina saw his hands tighten on the steering wheel—as if he were using a lot of control in letting her get away with that remark. But what difference did it make to him what she thought of Stella? Which thought gave rise to another question. 'Do you know Stella well?'

'You might say that,' he replied tightly, his voice growing louder. 'Before you go any further with your snide remarks, there's something you ought to know. Stella is——'

'Oh, I know what Stella is!' Gina cut him off completely—and blow the consequences! 'Stella is an over-dressed, over-perfumed man-eater!'

'Man——?' To her utter astonishment he threw back his head and laughed. Deep, rumbling laughter that was very genuine. 'Clearly you don't know Stella at all, and very clearly you dislike her.'

'Your powers of observation are amazing!' His laughter was irritating her. 'But you're wrong on the first count; I've spent enough time with her to form an opinion. And you might just as well know that she dislikes me as intensely as I dislike her.'

'Rubbish!' He was still laughing. It was another moment before he calmed down. 'It's a pity you feel like that, there's a great deal you could learn from Stella.'

'From *her*?'

'Yes,' he said firmly, suddenly serious. 'Like a little femininity for starters.'

It was a hurtful remark. It also clarified another one he'd made earlier on, when he'd been referring to her shortcomings as far as feelings were concerned. So he thought she fell short in the femininity stakes, too?

Silence reigned for quite a while after that. By now they had turned on to a road which was reasonably deserving of the name; at least it was smooth, if not signposted. She had no idea where they were, how far away from her father's home.

She kept her face turned away from her insulting, arrogant companion and concentrated on the scenery, consoling herself that she would soon be 'home'. At least then she would have some privacy. And, she hoped, a shower. And some sleep! Lots and lots of it.

The scenery became more interesting, even astonishing, as they rapidly covered ground. Barefooted women, some of whom were also bare-breasted, walked along the roadside balancing huge bundles on their heads, or baskets, or large clay urns. Men led animals along on ropes, children came scurrying out of mud huts or rickety-looking wooden houses with thatched roofs especially to wave at them as they sped past. The land was flat here, everything green tinged brown, as if the earth were parched for water. Gina looked up at the perfect blue of the sky; her father had told her it was the rainy season now, but there wasn't a hint of a bloud as far as the eye could see.

And then she saw a sign which read 'Malindi' and the town itself set about half a mile back off the road they were on. She couldn't see much detail, but she could see two large fairly smart-looking buildings which appeared to be hotels. Hotels? So people actually volunteered to come here for their holidays?

'You've missed the turning,' she said to Alex, thinking he must be daydreaming.

He said nothing. He just smiled. For the first time he smiled; a lazy, attractive smile which revealed beautifully even, enviably white teeth.

'Oh.' She felt a little foolish. 'My father's house isn't actually in the town, then?'

'No, it's on Watamu beach—another ten or fifteen minutes. It's a very beautiful spot, as I'm sure you'll agree.'

They were just skirting Malindi as he said that, and Gina was craning her neck to get a better look at the dusty, dreary little township. 'I shouldn't be too sure, Mr Craig. From what I've seen so far, this place isn't even living up to my expectations. And I certainly wasn't expecting much . . . It's a dump!'

She honestly expected him to agree with her, or at least to grant her another of his smiles. She couldn't have been more wrong—or more astonished, as he suddenly stepped on the brakes so hard that she slithered forward on a seat that was soaked in perspiration. It was only his vice-like grip on her shoulder that prevented her from shooting towards the windscreen.

'If you've deliberately set out to annoy me, you're making a damn good job of it!'

If she'd thought him angry before, it was nothing to the way he was now. He wasn't shouting, his voice was in

fact frighteningly quiet. No, it was his eyes that told her
of his fury. As Gina looked at him blankly, having no
idea why he was being like this, she saw that his eyes had
changed quite dramatically. They were lighter, brighter,
as blue and clear as a morning sky on a midwinter's day
in the Arctic. An involuntary shiver ran down her spine.

'You really push your luck, don't you?' he said, pushing
her back into her seat so hard that she winced from pain.
'First you speak to me as if I were an insolent servant,
then you insult Stella—which is tantamount to insulting
your father—and now, *now* you insult my country! Well,
you can count yourself lucky that you happen to be Harry
Duncan's daughter, and that I think so highly of him.
Otherwise I'd throw you out this minute and you'd walk
the rest of the way!'

Gina's eyes widened, big brown saucers in a pale-
skinned face which was growing whiter by the second. He
was Kenyan? Why had she assumed he was just another
tourist? She should have realised he was Kenyan from the
way he knew his way around on unsignposted roads, the
way he was so at home in that—that piece of cloth he
wore, many other examples of which she had seen on
people walking by the roadside. All this, not to mention
the depth of his tan, the way the sun had bleached his
hair and that very faint, almost indiscernible accent, so
vague that it couldn't be likened to anything. She had
thought it was just his way of speaking, the way the words
were slightly clipped—but no, she had heard it on the
plane; one of the stewardesses spoke that way.

Ye Gods! Was she doomed *always* to say the wrong
things to this man?

'Yes, I'm Kenyan!' he said, so irritated by her that he
wasn't even enjoying her embarrassment. 'And while this
country is not yet all that we want it to be, *we* like it.
Kindly remember that while you're gracing our soil with
your presence!'

Not another word was spoken until they turned into

the *shamba*—the land surrounding the house. Only then did he condescend to speak to her. He told her there were four African men employed at the house, that two of them looked after the land, that the land wasn't farmed in a serious way but contained a few coconut palms, limes and cashews.

'All the houses along this beach have a few acres surrounding them,' he said as they finally came to a halt. 'They were built on what used to be bushland.'

Gina said nothing. She was amazed that he'd cooled down so quickly. She was further surprised that he took the trouble to show her around.

As she stepped out on to the hot sand which served as a driveway around the property, two Africans wearing that now familiar beaming smile came hurrying towards the Land Rover.

'*Jambo, memsab—bwana!*' It was a chorus of welcome— at least, she thought it was a welcome.

Alex spoke back to them in their native Swahili, his voice easy but authoritative. They relieved Gina of her hand luggage, collected her suitcase and walked indoors ahead of her.

The 'house' turned out to be a bungalow, and it was not at all disappointing. The lounge was enormous, running the full length of the building and including a dining area. All the walls were white, the many louvred windows wide open. The floor was tiled, with a few rugs scattered here and there.

Over in one corner there was a bar built from wood, in another corner a very complex-looking stereo set, the speakers of which were positioned high up on the wooden rafters which bridged across the ceiling. Beyond them, the ceiling rose high up into a point. The furniture was cane, designed for comfort as well as coolness, since it was well cushioned. The wall lights were made from seashells and the decorations on the walls comprised a large, stuffed fish, two spears, a set of knives and a zebra skin.

There were no lamps, no paintings and no flowers or vases.

Gina was a little taken aback. This was definitely a masculine room. Where was the elegance she had expected of Stella? Then she noticed the dartboard, the fishing tackle on the floor, one of the bookshelves containing half a dozen games. She was even more taken aback. How quickly her father and Stella had adapted in this . . . this place to get bored in!

They stepped out of the far end of the lounge and were momentarily in the sunshine again. This area led to the verandah, which led to the bedrooms. There was a swimming pool, which was somewhat surprising since the sea was just a hundred yards away, across a white expanse of beach on which there wasn't a soul to be seen. There were hammocks, garden furniture, and the entire pool area was concreted and whitewashed. Beyond this area was a primitive garden abundant with bougainvillaea in lilacs, purple and flaming scarlet. Yellow acacia grew happily among clumps of wild flowers, the likes of which Gina had never seen before, and the air was heady with the scent of frangipani.

The view was magnificent, miles and miles of pure white sand and the splendour of the sparkling Indian Ocean. No, her father's house, at least, did not give Gina cause for further disappointment. If it weren't so unbelievably hot and sultry it would really be quite lovely—for a holiday.

Gina's bedroom was rather more luxurious than the lounge. There was a bathroom en suite, the bath being cut into the floor and made from green speckled tiles. The wardrobes ran from wall to wall and, for reasons she did not yet understand, had no doors on them. The bed was a double one and over it hung a mosquito net. She shuddered at the sight of it, but said nothing. All she really wanted now was to be alone. She wanted to bathe, unpack, flop on to the bed and sleep. She wanted Alex Craig out of her sight so she could rest her weary bones and get over her disappointment at her father's absence in private.

When Alex suggested they take a cold drink by the pool, however, she quickly jumped at the suggestion. She was still yearning for the drink she had never got on the plane. With her spirits now a little higher, knowing he would then leave, she could afford a little indulgence. As a matter of good manners, she decided, she would put up with him for another ten minutes or so while he had a drink; after all, he had been good enough to give her a lift from the airport—such as it was.

Gina took a seat under the shade of a bright red sun umbrella as Alex pushed his chair away from it, well into the glare of the roasting mid-afternoon sun. The two servants came out with glasses, a tall jug of iced lemonade and dishes of nuts, olives and fruits. Alex said something to them in their own tongue and they greeted Gina pleasantly in English. 'Meet Botana and Lanu,' he said to her.

'Pleased to meet you, memsab,' they chorused.

The older one proffered his hand as Gina was making a mental guess at their ages. They were both tall and good looking and Gina liked them instantly. It was in those split seconds that she heard the low, curt command from Alex Craig.

'Shake hands.'

As she was about to shake hands anyway, his remark evoked a quizzical look from her. He said nothing until the men padded away, barefooted, silent. Then she turned to him to find that he was scrutinising her carefully.

'Georgina, let me put you straight on this. Those men are your servants as long as you are in this house. They, and the other two, will do everything for you, anything you ask. But don't ever forget that they are Kenyan; this is their country and within their society they are honourable men with good, steady jobs. Treat them with respect.'

'But——' For a moment she didn't understand him.

Just what was he insinuating now? 'But of course!' She glared at him. Really! This man, this arrogant he-man who spoke to her so often as if she were thoroughly ill-bred and ill-educated, was becoming just too much to tolerate any longer. She had to get rid of him—and fast.

'Mr Craig, it's true that we've started off on the wrong footing. But let me assure you this is not the first time I've had servants to attend upon me, nor am I totally ignorant.'

He considered that for a moment. 'That isn't the impression you give. Dear girl, why are you so angry, so full of resentment? I'm trying to make you familiar with my country and the ways of it. I sincerely hope your stay here will be pleasant; I'm just trying to help you settle in.'

His face was impassive, his tone neutral so she couldn't tell whether he was being sarcastic or sincere. She was just about to give him the benefit of the doubt when he added, 'I treat as I find, Georgina Duncan. I find you ill-mannered, aggressive and rude, and I'm just warning you not to treat the servants like the haughty, tomboy brat that you are.'

Appalled, Gina shot to her feet so quickly that her chair clattered to the floor. 'Get out of here! Get *out*! Nobody, but *nobody* has ever spoken to me like that!'

Alex Craig leaned back in his seat and surveyed her, his eyes laughing at her with a mixture of mockery and distaste. 'Then it's high time somebody did. I told you, I treat as I find. Do as you would be done by, *Miss Duncan*. You annoyed me from the word go—and you haven't stopped annoying me since. If you want a civil conversation, then learn to speak in a civil tongue.'

'I want no conversation at all, Mr Craig!' she replied hotly. 'You've done your bit, given me a lift—for which I thank you—now kindly leave me in peace. If I never see you again, it will be too soon!'

'Dear girl, you'll be seeing a lot of me.' His grin was

wicked, infuriating, 'I'm holidaying here on Watamu beach. Besides,' he added for good measure, 'I promised your parents I'd look after you. Your father told me you'd grown a little wild of late—which I can well believe— and Stella asked me to entertain you. She thought you might be bored here.'

'How very thoughtful of her! Well, I've just released you from your promise—I can look after myself. So go and do your holidaying in your own house and spare me your visits to this place until my father gets back!'

And with that her head snapped up proudly. The nerve of the man! And what on earth had got into her father, saying she'd grown a 'little wild'? What was that supposed to mean?

Gina expected one final blasting from Alex Craig before it would be all over, before he would stalk out of the house and out of her life. She was prepared for it, the price she'd have to pay for her now desperate need for privacy and rest. She certainly wasn't prepared for what came next.

There was no verbal blasting from him, just a look of surprise as well-shaped blond eyebrows knitted together in a frown. And then came the lazy smile which told her he was suddenly enjoying himself like mad.

'We're certainly at cross purposes, Georgina. I don't know what your father told you, but you're definitely not up to date with the news. Your father's house is two miles farther up the beach. He's having extensive alterations made to it before he and Stella move in there. They've been staying here in the meantime, as *my* guests. So you see, you'll have to get used to having me around ... not only are you a guest in my country, you are also a guest in my home.'

CHAPTER TWO

SHE couldn't sleep. Whether it was over-exhaustion, the oppressive heat or the fact that Alex Craig's insults were continuing to needle her, Gina didn't know. Almost frantic with tiredness, she was unable to let go, to lose herself in the oblivion she so needed. The travelling alarm clock at the side of her bed told her it was almost seven o'clock. Alex had told her to join him for a sundowner before dinner at around nine. Just after dropping his bombshell he'd said that to her.

Bombshell, indeed! No wonder her mind was so active. Yes, Alex Craig was the cause of her sleeplessness. Alex Craig—and the knowledge that she was stuck here with him. For how long? It could be a week before her father got back. Maybe more! It was a depressing thought. She wished now that she'd stayed at home in London. At least Charles was in London . . .

Charles, and his long-standing proposal of marriage. Perhaps she should go home straight away, abandon the idea of talking to her father, abandon the idea of starting her own business—and accept Charles' proposal. She had a feeling she would accept it one day, in any case, not only because he was so persistent but because she knew for certain he was one man who was not influenced by the fact that she would some day inherit a fortune. Charles loved her for herself, just as she was.

But no! Gina smiled wryly at her own thoughts. Charles was charming, an aristocrat, reliable, dependable—but dull! Besides, she wanted more from life than settling in the role of an appendage to a man. Any man . . . Which meant that she had to stay here and wait for her father. Without his help and advice she couldn't put her business plans into action.

After travelling in a complete circle, Gina's thoughts were forced back to the problem of her arrogant host. She would steer clear of him. Let him get on with his 'holidaying', and make it her business to keep out of his way. But what about the inevitable meetings at mealtimes?

Her unfortunate remarks had given him entirely the wrong impression of her. To say he'd caught her in an off-moment was putting it mildly! For an instant, she considered trying to make a fresh start with him, explaining to him how bad the journey had been and how disappointed she was.

The idea was discarded as soon as it was considered. Firstly, she knew instinctively that Alex Craig would not change his opinion of her in a hurry. Secondly, she didn't honestly give a damn what he thought of her. And thirdly, he had more than repaid her tactless remarks with very cutting, *personal* insults towards her. And she was not going to forgive him for that.

Naturally, she could understand his reaction to her unfortunate appearance after her accident on the plane ... but he'd gone on to call her unfeminine, a tomboy. And that rankled. How it rankled! To have one's sexuality attacked is a very unpleasant experience, she acknowledged. Especially when the attack is made by one of the opposite sex, most especially by a man so overtly masculine and undeniably, wildly attractive.

Of course, she wasn't going to take it to heart; his remarks were entirely unfounded. Quite apart from Charles, hadn't there been sufficient admirers in college to assure her of her sexuality, her attractiveness? She'd done very little dating, true enough, but that was from choice, not from lack of opportunity. At the best of times Gina was easily bored, and she had not yet found a man who could hold her interest long enough to establish a lasting relationship. Charles couldn't really be counted because she had known him all her life, and he was more like one of the family, or rather, she was more like one of his family.

Nevertheless, she lingered a little longer than usual before the mirror that evening. Her simple, medium length hairstyle suited her, didn't it? Besides, it was practical. Blessed with a good complexion, if somewhat pale, she needed no make-up, so why bother with it? Her eyes were her best feature—dark brown, big and round, they gave her a look of innocence which suggested butter wouldn't melt in her mouth. There was nothing wrong with her figure, either. Of medium height and very slim, she was nicely in proportion except, perhaps, for her breasts which were maybe just a little too full. No, there was certainly nothing unfeminine about her.

Satisfied—and reassured—Gina slipped into a fresh pair of denims and a cotton shirt. To hell with Alex Craig and his insults. She would keep out of his way as much as possible. And when they shared a meal together, she would keep her distance. Yes, she would be distant, but polite. If he continued to 'treat as he found' then it would suit her down to the ground, and life would be more peaceful for both of them.

Having reached a satisfactory conclusion, Gina stepped out on to the verandah which ran halfway round the bungalow. To her delight, not to mention surprise, she could hear the faint strains of Beethoven's Moonlight Sonata as she approached the lounge.

For an instant she stood motionless at the entrance to the room. Alex's huge frame filled one of the armchairs, his long, muscular legs stretched out before him, bare feet supported by a stool. Still he wore a *kikoy*, albeit a different one—just a piece of plain brown cotton on which there was a vivid splash of orange, like a sun setting in a brown sea. His eyes were closed and he was oblivious to everything . . . everything but the music. The slight motion of his hands in keeping with the notes of the first, most poignant movement of the Sonata told her that. They were big hands, well shaped with scrupulously kept nails; and they denoted a certain sensitivity . . . a sensitivity she had seen nothing of.

With the eye of an artist Gina's gaze swept appreciatively over the strong, deeply-tanned body and the handsome, aristocratic profile, surprised to find him like this, so absorbed in the music of her own favourite composer. But while the artist in her couldn't help admitting he would make a fine subject for a painting, the woman in her rejected the idea. As a magnificent physical specimen, Alex Craig was perfect . . . as a person, she could think of no one less attractive.

When she moved, his eyes flew open instantly, sweeping over her quickly and yes, it was still there . . . with unconcealed disapproval. She said nothing until he moved over to the record deck and carefully lifted the record arm. 'No . . . don't do that.'

His smile was a strange one, accompanied by a brief shake of his head. Did he suppose she didn't care for the music—or was he not prepared to share it with her? Momentarily stuck for words, Gina resorted to a typically English comment about how hot it was.

'The rains are due,' he said. 'They were due four days ago, actually, but we're still waiting. It'll cool off when they come. It isn't normally this humid, I assure you.'

Gina looked at him in surprise. 'You mean you know almost to the day when the rains are due?'

His smile was indulgent. 'In this part of the country, yes. It's a serious business when they're late, as you can imagine. Which reminds me . . . keep your showers down to one a day, will you? All the houses along this beach are supplied by their own tanks. We're desperately low at the moment. Anyhow, there's a pool out there if you want to cool off during the day—not to mention the ocean.' He crossed over to the bar and looked at her expectantly. 'Gina, will you come into the room and stop hovering in the doorway? Sit down and tell me what you'd like to drink.'

She did as he bade her, noticing that he had ab-
breviated her name as she liked it.

'Beer, please.' So far, it seemed that he too had made a
similar resolve to the one she had made. Politeness was
the theme! But the thought was instantly dissolved when
he scoffed sarcastically at her choice of drink.

'Beer? And would you like one of my Havana cigars to
go with it?'

'No, thank you.' Her voice was stiff but she made no
retort to his sarcasm.

When he handed her the drink and sat down facing her
there was a strange few minutes' silence. It was very basic,
like two animals assessing one another, each trying to
gauge the strengths and weaknesses of the other. Gina's
nerve broke first.

'Mr Craig, I was——'

'A-a-ah!' He shook his head and wagged a finger at her
as if she were a naughty child. 'I've been addressing you
as you wish, kindly call me Alex.'

'Very well, Alex.' He was still managing to annoy her,
but she had made a resolve and would stick to it. 'I was
about to comment that I can't see my father settling
here.'

'Your father loves it here!' he said dismissively. 'Stella
says she's never seen him so relaxed. The climate is good
for him. There's been a big improvement in his health
since he's been here.'

'You know about his condition, then?'

'His heart, the angina? Yes, I know about it.'

Again there was a pause, but this time it was only Gina
who was making an assessment. Apart from his bluntness,
Alex Craig was so very different from her father.

'How long have you known Daddy?'

'About seven years.'

'Really? He's never mentioned you to me.'

'He's mentioned you to me.' He smiled—that wildly
attractive, slow smile. But Gina had learned by now that

it usually preceded one of his more unpleasant remarks.
'He told me he had a lovely daughter...' He was leaving the rest unsaid, for what it was worth. His puzzled,
deliberately puzzled, expression said the rest for him.

'Did you do business together?' she asked.

'Uh-huh. And here in Africa he's consulted me on a
few matters. Like the mine, for instance.'

'The mine?' This was news to Gina. 'What mine?'

Alex seemed surprised. 'Didn't you know he's invested
heavily in a copper mine? It isn't actually in Kenya,
it's——'

'No, I didn't!' Gina was annoyed. It wasn't very nice
to be told of major things such as this by a stranger.

'Well, I'm sure he'll tell you all about it when you see
him.'

At that point Botana appeared in the far entrance. Alex
nodded to him. 'Are you ready to eat, Gina?' Ready? She
was starving! 'All right, Botana. Five minutes.'

In that five minutes Gina tried to find out a little more
about her host, but he seemed unwilling to talk about
himself. When she asked him what he did for a living, he
told her he was just a simple farmer.

'A simple farmer? This place is your holiday home, you
drive an Aston Martin, and you tell me you're a simple
farmer. Come off it!'

'Ah,' he laughed then. 'You saw the car parked under
the trees?'

'Yes, when we arrived.'

'And aren't you dying to ask why I didn't collect you
from the airport in it?'

'Yes, I'm dying to.' She couldn't help smiling at that.
'But I won't.'

And then his eyes were sparkling with laughter, crinkl-
ing at the sides. And very nice it was, too. So different
from his insolent smile. 'Because I picked up a six-inch
nail in the front offside tyre on my way back from driving
your parents to the airport. You have Harry's builders to

thank for the lift in the Land Rover. And that . . . dear girl . . . is the first time I've seen you smile. It's a vast improvement. You really should try it more often. Shall we eat?'

Gina was imagining all sorts of unlikely food being placed before her and was very pleasantly surprised by the dinner. They started with chilled melon, followed by a huge platter of fillet steaks and a large bowl of crisp, fresh salad in a delicious dressing. She ate ravenously and when she finally put down her knife and fork she looked up to find Alex Craig watching her, his eyes dancing with laughter.

'I must say it's good to see someone tucking in so heartily.' He gave a short nod, as if he were pleased. 'Skinny little thing, aren't you?'

Gina smiled at him, trying to appear unperturbed. 'You're a master at giving the backhanded compliment, Alex. The dinner was super. Thank you.' She added the thanks as an afterthought, determined to stick to her resolve and not let him goad her.

'You have Stella to thank,' he informed her then. 'She's been giving Botana a few lessons. His cooking was very— basic—before Stella came here. She's a superb cook.' Then, with unmistakable admiration he added, 'She's a gorgeous woman. She's *all woman*, if you know what I mean. I knew she'd make the perfect wife for Harry.'

'The perfect wife?' Gina couldn't have disagreed with him more. 'And just what is your definition of the perfect wife?'

Alex looked slightly surprised by the question, as if she should know the answer. 'A woman who's faithful and loyal, who puts her husband before herself. A woman who is all things to her man—supportive, a companion, hostess, friend, mistress . . .'

'And servant?'

'No, that isn't a word I——'

'What you're describing to me is a mindless creature

whose entire existence is dedicated to the comfort and well-being of "her man"; merely an extension of the man.'

'Not at all.'

Gina's smile was derisive. 'Then what about the woman as an individual, a person who has a career of her own, for example?'

'Marriage is a career in itself,' he reasoned. 'I see both parties as individuals, but individuals making up a whole. It's a partnership that needs to be constantly worked at, never taken for granted.'

With difficulty Gina held back her retort. She disliked his ideas and it would have been very easy to shoot them down in flames. But for the sake of peace, she let the conversation drop. Or tried to.

'I take it you're anti-marriage, Gina?'

She considered that for a moment. 'No. Let's just say that I want more from life than being subservient to a man. It seems to me that marriage involves too many compromises. I should insist on retaining my own individuality, my own friends. If I ever find myself considering such a step, I'm sure it will be because I have nothing better to do. And that's a long way off—a long way!'

Alex grimaced. 'You've got some very strange ideas. However, I take it from your last remark that you've got your life neatly mapped out?'

'I—have plans. Yes.' She was not prepared to say any more. The plans she had were tentative, dependent entirely upon her father. If he didn't approve of what she had in mind, she would be left drifting. It was a dreadful thought. The trouble was that she didn't really know what she wanted to do, and just thinking about the future brought on that nervousness which had plagued her of late.

Alex was about to refill their wineglasses, but Gina declined. Superb though it was, the heady red wine, the beer and the humidity were combining to resurrect her headache. Was it that, or the fact that she couldn't relax and be herself? Having constantly to watch her words was becoming quite a strain.

'How come you didn't go to their wedding?' Alex was eyeing her over the rim of his glass.

'I—I beg your pardon?' There was a distinct note of accusation in his voice.

'You heard me. How come you didn't attend your father's wedding?'

'Because,' she said coolly, thinking it none of his business, 'I was given two days' notice—by telegram—and I didn't think that a very courteous invitation. There was also the fact that I'd have had to fly across the Atlantic.'

'So what? It was during the summer, so it wasn't as if you'd needed to take time off college. How come you didn't make the effort?'

The conversation was becoming increasingly irritating, and Gina's resolve was slowly slipping away. She didn't care for his attitude—and it was none of his business, anyway. 'How come you know so much about it?'

'Because I was there. After all, I was responsible for it. It was I who introduced your father to Stella.'

That little piece of information didn't go down at all well. 'So you're responsible for the sudden rush of love in bloom!' she said recklessly. 'Well, I'm sure Stella is very grateful to you for finding her a *third* husband. Let's hope she does make the perfect wife—this time!'

Alex's mouth formed a straight line, his eyes sparking with annoyance. 'I'm well aware that Stella's had two unfortunate previous marriages. And I'll thank you to curb your vicious tongue where she's concerned.'

Silence reigned after that, until Botana came in with coffee and they moved over by the windows where there was just the faintest breeze. The atmosphere was strained, unpleasant. Gina was aware that her last remark about Stella was continuing to annoy Alex, but she didn't give a hoot. All she wanted was to drink her coffee and go to bed. She couldn't remember ever feeling as physically tired as she did now.

She had made an effort, but she simply couldn't get on with this man. Almost everything he said was punctuated by sarcasm. She disliked the way his mind worked, his chauvinistic attitude. When he asked her if she'd care to go water-skiing in the morning, she instantly declined.

'The tide will be perfect,' he said persuasively. 'We can get up early and——'

'Alex, I'm tired, very tired. I intend to sleep late in the morning, okay? I shall be in no mood for water-skiing.'

He shrugged. 'Perhaps we'll go fishing in the afternoon, then.'

'I can think of nothing more boring. Look, Alex, you just get on with your holiday. Kindly leave me to my own devices.' She was not going to let him organise her time. Besides, something in her bones told her there would be an almighty row if she spent too long in his company.

'And what about my promise to your parents?' He was goading her, she knew it, even though his face was impassive.

'We've already settled that. And would you stop including Stella as one of my parents?'

'I see.' He reached for a cigarette then, one eyebrow slightly arched as he surveyed her through a thin haze of smoke. 'I begin to get your measure, Gina. Everything I accused you of earlier today was right. Now I see also that you have an unhealthy attachment to your father and an unreasonable dislike of your stepmother because she's stolen him away. Rather childish, don't you think?'

'That's ridiculous!' She slammed down her coffee cup with a resounding crack, resenting him more than ever. But somewhere deep inside her his words struck home. There was nothing unhealthy about her attachment to her father, of course, and Alex Craig had no right to say such a thing. But she did resent Stella for taking him away . . .

It was that, and only that, which made her sit still
when she would otherwise have walked out of the room.
She didn't want to add to Alex's opinion that she was
childish by running away from him. Nor did she want to
let him see that, in part, he had hit upon the truth.

Damn him! Damn his sarcasm, his bluntness, his
shrewdness and, worst of all, that awful way he had of
making her feel so selfconscious, unreasonable. She didn't
think much of herself at the best of times, without him
hammering home her shortcomings!

Alex Craig was silent, smoking his cigarette, watching
her almost as if he could read her mind. Gina felt a blush
rising from the base of her throat. Why, why did she get
so disturbed when he watched her like that? Why was it
that he made her feel so—so inadequate?

But he hadn't finished with her yet. 'What I said is
true, Gina. You should be able to see it for yourself. For a
well-educated girl you don't know much, do you? Even
allowing for the fact that you're fourteen years my junior,
I find you ... immature, to say the least. For someone
who's studying art you're surprisingly lacking in percep-
tion. For someone who's had the benefit of a Swiss finishing school, your manners and appearance are appalling.
Is that how they taught you to sit, with one ankle hooked
over a knee, wearing an attitude and clothes more befit-
ting a youth? Is that where they taught you to drink beer?
What happened to those nice finishing touches, the charm
and the little refinements—like your stepmother has? Or
are you just going through a——'

It was more than she could take. More than she would
allow her own father to say to her! She shot to her feet,
furious with him.

'All right, Mr Craig, that's enough! You've taken my
measure and you don't like what you see. Well, that's fine
by me. From now on just keep out of my way. Mind
your own business and keep your opinions to yourself!'

The only trouble was that in order to get out of the

room she had to get past the coffee table—and him. Her dignified exit was ruined when his hand shot out and grabbed her firmly by the wrist.

'I see I've hit target with quite a few home truths tonight.' His eyes narrowed speculatively as he held her in place with a vice-like grip. 'Why are you so unhappy, Gina? Why so defensive? What's eating at you?'

'Go to hell!'

She didn't regret her words, even as his grip tightened against the fragile bones of her slender wrist. And then he was smiling, a sudden flash of white amid the strong, tanned features. 'You've got spirit, I'll grant you that much. Ah, but on the whole I'm so disappointed, you see. I thought I was going to have a charming, pretty playmate to keep me company while Harry's away.'

'You make me sick!' she hissed, struggling frantically to get away from him. It was impossible. Even as he sat, his one hand was keeping her at heel. 'You are the perfect chauvinist, Alex Craig. You're the epitome of everything I dislike in a man—arrogant, self-opinionated and fixed with the old-fashioned idea that women were put on this earth for man's pleasure. Well, I don't think that way. I am who I am. I make no apology for it, and if you don't like it—tough!'

He got to his feet slowly, still holding her, still smiling, impervious to her insults. 'Just as I thought, a rebel in blue jeans! I know what ails you, Gina, even if you don't. You don't know *who* you are, what you want. You've not yet come alive to the fact that you're a woman. You need a man who'll——'

She swore at him then. Wriggling frantically to get away from him as perspiration broke out on her skin, she spat out a stream of abuse which surprised even herself.

'Why, you little wildcat! I'll teach you to be so aggressive!'

'What are you *doing*?' she shrieked, frightened as she saw his eyes change colour, grow lighter, as they had done

before when he was really mad at her. She'd gone too far,
and she knew it.

'I'll teach you to swear at me!' The deep tones of his
voice were vibrant with anger as he half dragged her towards the chair. 'I'm going to do something your father
should have done years ago—see how you like a good
spanking!'

It was thanks only to the perspiration on her arms that
Gina was able to slip out of his grasp. She bolted from the
room as fast as her legs would carry her, terrified that
he'd run after her. But as she slammed her bedroom door
behind her, it was only the sound of his laughter that
pursued her.

She stood with her back against the door, her heart
pounding, her face aflame with humiliation and indignation. How dared he! How dared he treat her like that!
He'd never dare behave like that if her father were here.
Just wait! She'd tell her father all about Alex Craig—and
then see what their friendship was worth!

The very childishness of the thought pulled her up
short. How could she report him to her father? Harry
would probably laugh at her. She was, after all, nineteen
years old. And Alex Craig was *her* problem. If she couldn't
handle him, then the lack was hers. Damn the man! Damn
her bad luck at being thrust into his company like this.
Damn his stupid, chauvinistic ideas!

Had the mosquito net not been draped neatly around
the bed, Gina would have thrown herself on to it and
sobbed out her frustrations. This day had been disastrous.
The journey, the bad news, the choking, impossible heat—
and *him*! Her hateful brute of a host who was hardly more
than an animal.

She tore off her shirt and flung it on a nearby chair.
She couldn't even have a shower to cool herself off.
Trembling with anger, she marched into the bathroom.
Surely a basinful of water wouldn't affect the water short-
age too much!

She had got as far as putting the plug in the basin when she suddenly let out a terrified, ear-piercing scream which echoed around the entire bathroom before fading off into stark, stony silence.

Gina stood stock still. Petrified, hardly able to believe her eyes. From out of the overflow of the sink there had appeared a large black head belonging to a thing—some *thing* which was now wriggling its way to freedom, curling its way around one of the taps as the rest of its body emerged. It was dull, pitch black, with two antennae on its head which were twitching revoltingly. It was flat, about three inches wide at the widest point, and about ten inches in length, and its entire body was covered in a million fine short hairs which were now standing on end.

If anyone had told her she'd be glad to see Alex Craig again, she would never have believed it. But when she became aware that he was standing behind her, then, and only then, did her heart start to function again, pounding against her ribs in protest as she gulped in huge lungfuls of air.

'Don't move,' he said quietly. His hand came out to touch her shoulder, as if seeking an acknowledgment. 'Don't move a muscle. Those things can shift like lightning.'

Gina did as he said, oblivious to the fact that she was half naked, trying only to suppress the hysteria rising within her. Alex backed away from her slowly, silently. Within seconds he was edging past her, one of the heavy shoes she'd travelled in gripped tightly in his right hand.

When he struck the insect at an incredible speed there was a nauseating squelch as a spurt of dark red blood splattered over the basin. It didn't die easily. It took two more belts before its head and tail-end stopped wriggling. Then Alex grabbed a hand-towel, gathered what was left of the creature into it and carelessly chucked it out of the window. Without turning, he started rinsing the sink, scrubbing his hands. And all the time, he was talking, half-laughing. '. . . unfortunate experience for you. Never in all my days in Africa have I seen one of those things inside a house. Don't get them inland . . . Hairs on the back are poisonous. Won't kill, but very, very nasty . . .'

Gina hadn't moved an inch. She had barely heard him. She knew from the blurred vision of him, the ringing in her ears, that she was going to faint. It was only when a strangled cry escaped from her that Alex turned.

'Hey . . . take it easy!' And then his arms were around her, her head being held gently against a warm, firm shoulder. She was aware only of his strength, its comfort, and within seconds she was feeling better. She became aware of something on her back hurting as Alex's arms held her firmly against him. It was seconds before she became aware of her nakedness, her breasts brushing against his bare chest . . .

'I—I'm all right now.' When she finally found her voice it was so thick with embarrassment it was barely audible. 'Let me go, Alex, I'm all right.'

He let her go, steadying her on her feet but keeping his hands on her shoulders as if unsure of her strength.

'It's okay, Gina,' he said with more gentleness than she had ever heard him use. 'I don't know how that thing got in there—or out of it—but it won't happen again, I'm sure of it. I'm sorry you had to see that.'

Gina lowered her head, unable to meet his eyes, her hands and arms automatically reaching up to cover her breasts.

He put a hand under her chin and tilted her head upwards. 'It's a little late to worry about that,' he smiled. 'Don't let it throw you.'

But Gina couldn't make a joke out of it—any of it. 'Please leave me now,' she muttered.

When Alex took hold of her hands and put them by her sides, holding them there, she didn't resist. She couldn't fight now. She was just too weary, too upset, too disgusted with this day and all that had happened in it. If

Alex Craig wanted to take this opportunity of kicking her while she was down, then let him. She closed her eyes and waited, her face burning with humiliation. Nothing happened. He didn't move, he didn't speak.

When she tentatively opened her eyes she found him smiling at her—without malice, without mockery. Deep blue eyes held her transfixed, almost hypnotised as his face came nearer until he was kissing her. Gently, briefly his lips brushed against hers in a kiss that was almost chaste. 'You hide your light under a bushel, dear Gina. You hide behind a disguise.'

He stepped away from her, his eyes travelling over her face, her throat, along the contours of her body to her breasts, the tiny waist and slender hips encased in tight blue jeans. Still there was no laughter, no criticism, just a strange sentence before he left her alone, 'You're a very beautiful girl . . . if only you would allow yourself to realise it, to enjoy it.'

He left her standing there motionless, dumbstruck. The fingers of one hand came up to brush against her lips, to try to stop the tingling that was the aftermath of his kiss. While her mind recoiled from it, her body relived the memory of a very tender kiss, the feeling of comfort as she was locked against that magnificent chest, her breasts pressing close . . .

Gina shook her head as if to stave off an unpleasant dream. Something odd was happening to her, and she didn't like it. Alex Craig had provoked all sorts of questions in her mind, questions about herself which she must examine and re-examine. He'd shaken her to her very foundations, and she resented it. Worse, some gossamer-thin veil had been lifted. Despite her loathing for Alex Craig as a person, she had become physically aware of him. No longer would she be able to appreciate his looks with merely the eye of an artist.

CHAPTER THREE

IT was a strange sort of pattern they fell into during the next few days. Perhaps it was because they saw little of each other that their conversations became slightly more amiable, Gina wasn't sure. Certainly they stuck to safe, neutral subjects and spoke quite a lot about Harry—who was the only person they really had in common.

Gina went to bed each evening after dinner, still trying to get in a full night's sleep. She didn't succeed. Each night, in the early hours, she wandered on to the patio around the swimming pool and sat quietly in the hammock, enjoying the silence and the huge orange moon set against a background of twinkling stars on a black velvet base, like an enormous collage. Always there was the steady buzz of night creatures, the rhythmic hum of mosquitos, some of which had made acquaintance with her ankles and brought up soft pink swellings. But that didn't bother her; it was the heat which kept her awake.

When she did sleep, it was usually from sometime before sunrise to mid-morning, when it was coolest. Alex was never there when she got up and breakfasted on mangoes and paw-paw, the delicious fruits she had quickly grown to adore. Sometimes she would see him as he sped along the surface of the ocean on his water-skis, with one or other of the servants handling the speedboat. It looked like a lot of fun, although she had declined Alex's offer of being taught how to do it.

She had also declined the fishing trips, the invitation to join him for a drink after dinner in one of the hotels farther down the beach. He told her he was giving a few lessons in scuba diving to some of the hotels' residents—and she had refused to join in that activity, too.

Her boredom, therefore, was entirely of her own making. She played records, she wrote home, she played Patience, and she read a lot. She wanted to avoid the sun—and Alex Craig—as much as possible. For days she had been mulling over his cryptic comments in her bedroom that first evening. She wanted to ask him what he had meant, but her pride would not allow that. Her feelings about Alex had become very mixed, confused. She disliked him, but for some obscure reason she was fascinated by him. She resented his bluntness—yet respected a man who spoke his mind, like her father did.

Underlying all this was a deeper resentment because she was aware of him physically. She resented that because it somehow made her vulnerable, especially since she could never wield that same power over him. He had made it perfectly plain what he thought of her as a woman!

It was on the morning of the fifth day when Alex became impatient with her. Gina had just started a letter to Charles when she looked up to find Alex standing in the doorway. He stood with his head held high, feet set apart in that stance she found somewhat intimidating. But it was something more than nervousness which made her stomach contract slightly at the sight of him. He looked magnificent, wearing just a pair of white swim trunks which accentuated the golden colour of his skin and hugged tightly against narrow hips leading to the flat, taut muscles of his stomach. He was still wet from his skiing, the heat and the steady rise and fall of his chest causing the water to run down in small rivulets amid the mass of blond hair on his chest.

His face was set, unsmiling, but Gina couldn't miss the mocking laughter in his eyes as her gaze swept over him.

'Can you drive, Gina?' Such was his surprising opening gambit as he walked over to the bar.

'Yes. Why?'

He threw a bunch of keys towards her. 'Because I want

you to go into Malindi and check the post.' He helped himself to a drink as she muttered something about not realising the post had to be collected.

He came and sat beside her, just a little too close for comfort. 'It does, dear girl. We don't have nice little red vans delivering letters in this part of the world. Open your hand.' He pointed to the various keys, his fingers brushing against her open palm in a way that seemed—almost intimate.

Ye gods, what had got into her? She pulled herself up short and nodded as he talked to her. 'Yes, I've got it. Door and ignition, boot key, Post Office box key.'

'Okay. There might just be a letter from Harry and Stella. I reckon since they haven't phoned, they might have dropped us a line, or a telegram. And while you're in town, would you mind getting some food? We're running short.'

'Oh—of course. What do you want?'

'I rather thought I'd leave that up to you. Botana has to be told explicitly about meals, and how to cook them, so you'd better buy stuff you know how to cook.' He raised an eyebrow and looked at her sardonically. 'Unless, of course, you're such a liberated woman that you only know about opening cans?'

She left straight away, following Alex's instructions for finding the little town. It was perfectly straightforward, just a case of making a couple of turnings, then following her nose. It was pleasant, driving in the blue open-topped Aston Martin, with the warm wind caressing her skin. She was quite flattered that Alex had trusted her so readily with a car which must have cost a fortune to import.

It was a curious shopping expedition. There was no letter from her father, much to her disappointment. But there was nothing she could do about that. She didn't have his number in Australia, but surely he would ring her soon, tell her what was happening?

Half an hour later, the cold box in the boot of the car

was filled with meat. Gina had communicated her wants by the international language of pointing to things in the butcher's shop. As she did in the vegetable market. In the newer section of town, however, many of the shopkeepers spoke English, and to Gina's surprise she found that there was available everything she needed—even a little news-agents where they sold sketch pads, pencils and charcoal. Gina armed herself with these, unable to resist them, got an ice lolly from the fridge and ate it rapidly before it melted on her way to the chemist's.

Within an hour the back seat and boot of the car was filled to capacity with food, vegetables, cartons of soft drinks and a crate of red wine Alex had been very specific about buying.

She drove slowly out of town down a narrow street which was lined with stalls, their owners shouting friendly greetings to her and urging her to buy. Some of the passers-by stopped to stare at the car, others actually stroked it as she drove carefully past them, much to her amusement. On an impulse she stopped at the very last stall and for a few Kenyan shillings bought three *kangas*, allowing the outsized African lady to show her how they should be tied. There was a lot of laughter and a lot of arm-waving and jabbering before Gina got the hang of it. It was in high spirits that she set off for Watamu, making a mental note to wear something on her head the next time she ventured outdoors for so long.

Alex was sprawled out on the settee when she got back, smoking one of his occasional cigarettes and eyeing her critically as she walked into the room and made a beeline for the bar.

'Did you get on okay?'

'Yes, it was fun, actually. Botana's putting everything away. I got the wine you wanted.' Gina helped herself to a beer and smiled over at him.

'We're going to a barbecue this evening,' he told her

then. 'The Easter crowd has arrived at the Marlin and the Seafarers. It'll be fun.'

Gina hesitated. 'No, I don't think so. I'd rather have an early night, thanks anyway.'

He looked at her sharply. 'I'm not asking, Gina—this time I'm telling you. You're coming with me. I'm sick of seeing you moping round this place. I've given you time to acclimatise; you're still as pale as the day you arrived—and you've got the stamina of a ninety-year-old!'

'Alex, you don't have to feel obliged——'

'Obliged, hell!' he snapped. 'You're boring me, Gina. You'll get out and do something for a change.'

Annoyance swept over her. 'I'm perfectly happy as I am!'

'Oh, yes?' He got to his feet and pointed to the letter she had begun to Charles. 'It's no use telling people this place is boring, if you don't do anything about it!'

Shocked, she plonked her drink down on the bar, her arms waving about in agitation. 'Have you been reading my letter?'

'I could hardly help it, you left it on view right there on the table!' He was half shouting at her, but she could tell he wasn't really annoyed. Not half as much as she was.

'Come and have a swim before lunch,' he said then.

'No.'

'Gina . . .'

Laughter bubbled up inside her as he came towards her menacingly, walking as if he were a robot, arms stuck out straight in front of him.

'No!' She squealed, dashing from behind the bar and running round the dining table. 'I don't want to swim. I can't! No . . . Alex . . . Alex!'

It was no good. Within five seconds she was over his shoulder in a fireman's lift and he was carrying her towards the swimming pool. She fought and wriggled, yelping loudly until her voice faded off in mid-air and she was thrown into the deep end of the water.

She surfaced, gagging and spluttering, the water dragging at her white cotton jeans, pulling her down again.

Alex was laughing his head off. 'Swim!' he yelled at her. 'Let me see you *do* something. Swim, girl, swim!'

'I can't!' she spluttered, her breath coming in gasps because she hadn't got used to the coldness of the water. 'Really! *I can't!*' She waited just long enough to see the dawning, horrified look on his face as he dived in after her. Then she dropped beneath the water and swam like mad to the other side of the pool.

Alex surfaced behind her instantly. 'Why, you little . . .!' He roared with laughter. 'You really had me fooled!' He moved swiftly then, his arms coming up. Gina saw she was in for a ducking and held her back rigid, standing her ground, which only served to amuse him more.

'Smart little devil, aren't you?'

'Yes,' she said, with wide-eyed innocence, appearing not to move while she hooked a leg around his and threw him off balance. He went down—but he took her with him, his arms locked around her back. They were both gasping when they came up, their faces only inches apart.

There followed a strange few seconds. Gina saw the laughter fading from his eyes, his face became dead serious as he held her tightly against him, the water lapping gently against their bodies. She felt the pulses pounding in her ears, felt the long, deep breath Alex took just before he stepped away from her.

'I—think you'd better put on a costume or something,' he said quietly, and when she followed the line of his gaze it was to see her nipples standing prominently, the dark shadow of them showing plainly through the wet cotton of her white blouse.

She flushed with embarrassment, hating herself for responding so readily, hating the tell-tale signs her body made. Even more, she hated Alex for moving away from

her when she'd wanted him to kiss her. Did he find her so
unfeminine that he could very easily dismiss her like that?

Gina was still thinking about the incident when she was
dressing for the barbecue that evening. Dressing? It was
merely a question of slipping into a pair of sandals, briefs,
and wrapping the gaily-coloured *kanga* around herself. She
tied it firmly between her breasts—and sat down before
the mirror in a state of perplexity. Who was she trying to
kid? She wasn't wearing her new purchase for herself, her
own comfort . . . she'd put it on in the hope that she
would impress Alex Craig!

Swearing beneath her breath, Gina pulled a wry face
at herself in the mirror. She'd never pandered to a man
in her life! What game was this? Charles didn't evoke this
sort of nonsense, nor did he expect it of her. He loved her
just the way she was; he admired her independence, her
individuality, respected her opinions about the male/
female roles in life.

But Alex Craig did not. He was fourteen years older
than she, and thought very differently. He spoke of the
likes of Stella as if she were God's gift to mankind, the
way she dressed, her talents for cooking, her elegance, her
charm. And as for his ideas about marriage . . .! Yet, perversely, it was him she was trying to impress. He had got
to her somehow. That strange remark about her hiding
herself behind a disguise . . . the way he had maligned her
femininity, called her a tomboy, even. She wanted to
prove him wrong, wrong!

She gathered together her beach bag and towel, knowing it stupid to be affected by Alex but unable to deny
that she found him a challenge. His rejection of her in the
pool today hadn't helped matters, either. She wanted to
make him acknowledge her as a sexually attractive
woman, to prove a point both to herself and to him. He'd
made her feel inadequate, and she wanted to make him
eat his words. Perhaps it was stupid, but what fun it would

be to make him physically aware of her, to have him in her power and then suddenly switch off! And then she'd tell the arrogant chauvinist never again to judge a book by its cover!

It was with a small sense of achievement that she walked into the lounge and saw Alex's eyes flick over the soft swell of her breasts, accentuated in the most flattering way by the knot which was holding the *kanga* in place.

'Ah, I'd had the impression that your entire wardrobe was made up of jeans. So you're beginning to get the feel of Africa, at last?' He drained his glass and stood up, dressed in a pair of leather sandals and hip-hugging pale blue shorts.

'Oh, I picked it up on the market today,' Gina said nonchalantly. 'Thought it'd be more comfortable than slacks.'

'Cooler, too,' he agreed. 'Very sensible. Shall we go?'

The barbecue was fun. It was held on the beach directly in front of the Marlin Hotel. Everyone contributed several bottles of wine and the rate of consumption was vast. There was food enough to feed an army, but it, too, disappeared at an astonishing rate.

The palm trees skirting the hotel were lit up with coloured lights, and the spillage of light from the hotel's lounge bar made the atmosphere perfect. A couple of lads were playing guitars and singing, and it wasn't long before everyone joined in. Several couples were dancing on the sand and there was a lot of laughter and gaiety. There was a soft breeze blowing in from the sea, which just took the edge off the otherwise stifling humidity.

It was only when it got to midnight that Gina wished she'd stayed in the bungalow. At midnight Mandy appeared, and Gina lost Alex completely.

'Hello, darling!' The voice belonged to a tall, long-legged blonde who was wearing a red bikini, so brief that it left nothing at all to the imagination. Around her waist and neck she wore several gold chains, around her wrist a solid gold charm bracelet which jangled as she undulated along the sand. Her tan was so deep she was mahogany-coloured; the movement of her hips exaggerated, as was the green eye-shadow around her tawny-coloured eyes. Eyes which were lit up as she greeted Alex, and somewhat resentful as she was introduced to Gina.

'Meet my neighbour,' said Alex, smiling down at Gina who was sitting cross-legged on her towel. 'This is Mandy Miller. Mandy—meet Gina.'

The two women nodded at one another and Mandy coiled herself neatly on to Alex's beach towel. He grinned as he lowered himself next to her.

'Neighbours?' Gina said lightly. 'You live around here?'

'No, no!' Mandy tossed back shoulder-length curly hair and laughed huskily. 'We're neighbours in Nairobi. I live about five miles away from Alex's plantation. It might sound a long way to you, but I'm his nearest neighbour. You're English, I take it?'

Alex answered for her. 'Yes. Mandy, this is Harry Duncan's daughter. You've heard me speak of him.'

'Often.' She nodded, turning to appraise Gina openly and coolly. 'I just got here today, thought I'd come for the Easter break. Anyway, the gossip was waiting for me when I arrived—as always—and I hear your father and his wife have been called away—gone to New Zealand or something. So you and Alex have been thrust into one another's company, eh?'

'Australia, actually.' Gina's voice was as cold as ice. She resented the innuendo in Mandy's last sentence. And she resented this intrusion of what she'd hoped would be her first really successful few hours with Alex Craig.

When Alex went to get more drinks, Mandy's resentment of Gina was made very plain indeed. 'You must be quite chuffed with yourself,' she began cattily, 'living with Kenya's most eligible bachelor.'

'Staying with him, if you don't mind. I am a guest in

his house, yes. And as for his eligibility, I wouldn't know—or care.'

'I see,' she said, disbelief very clear in her eyes. 'You wouldn't know that he owns one of the biggest coffee plantations in Nairobi? That he's just spent half a million pounds on a drinks factory in Mombasa? That he's looking for a wife, and doesn't mind saying so?'

Gina was taken aback by this—all of it. Alex had been reluctant to talk about himself to her, hadn't even told her what sort of 'farming' he did. He certainly hadn't told her he was looking for a wife! But then why should he tell her, of all people?

'No, I didn't know any of that,' Gina said firmly. 'And quite frankly, Miss Miller, I'm not impressed. Neither money nor marriage interests me.'

'Ah, yes, but then you're a rich man's daughter. I forgot.' Mandy laughed then, as if it would lessen the sting in her words and make them acceptable. 'And perhaps you're a little young to qualify for Alex's list of potential wives. If he has one.' The last remark was added sullenly, leaving Gina in no doubt that Mandy thought herself very well qualified—but making very little progress.

It didn't seem that way to Gina, though, when Mandy turned on the charm on Alex's return and monopolised his attention completely. The following hour was quite educational for Gina, even though she was disgusted at Mandy Miller's behaviour. How could she demean herself like that, flattering him and flirting with him outrageously?

Telling herself that she would never go to those lengths to win a man's attention, Gina watched the other girl's performance with something which bordered on appalled fascination. Mandy moved a lot, posing her body to its best advantage, stretching out her long legs against the sand, putting her fingers around Alex's as he lit her cigarettes and leaning forward as she did so, giving him the best possible view of her ample breasts.

'Gina, where've you gone?' Alex was looking at her quizzically. 'You've dropped out of the conversation entirely.'

Of course she had! Mandy Miller had seen to that, with her constant chatter and her quest, her successful quest, to keep Alex's eyes on her curvaceous body.

'Slight headache, that's all,' Gina said truthfully. She did have a slight headache, though she'd only just become aware of it.

'Too much wine?' Alex smiled at her like an indulgent older brother, much to Mandy's amusement.

'Not at all,' she bristled. 'It's because there's a storm in the air.'

'Oh, really?' Mandy's voice was cynical as she exposed the long curve of her throat in a big display of looking up at the sky. A sky that was as clear as glass. There wasn't a cloud in sight and the stars were twinkling like huge cut diamonds.

'What are you, some sort of witch?' Alex laughed in disbelief while Mandy's low, throaty laugh tried unsuccessfully to hide her irritation. 'Alex darling, I think this is Miss Duncan's way of telling you she wants to go home.'

'Not at all . . .' Gina began. But Mandy had given up, for this evening at least. Whatever plans she had had in mind for Alex had been stymied by Gina's presence. Her next remark made it abundantly clear that she wasn't intending to waste the entire weekend, however. 'I'm staying in the usual chalet,' she purred, as Alex got to his feet. 'Pop in any time. I'll be here until next Tuesday.' Then, in an elaborate display of brushing sand off her bikini bra, 'Come and have a drink with me—if you can get time off from your babysitting obligations . . . Goodnight, Miss Duncan, it was lovely to meet you.'

Failing to make a quick, adequate retort left Gina bristling with anger. She marched over the sands, around

the hotel to the car park at a breakneck pace. Alex's infuriating, gorgeous, insolent smile when he sidled up to
her only made her more angry. 'What are you smiling
at?'

'Dear girl, what's upsetting you?' His laughter was
deep, low.

'Her! That—that horrible woman. What a nerve!'

'Mandy? Why, she's a lovely girl. She's been a good
friend to me.'

'Friend?' Gina scoffed. 'She'd like to be more than that!
Or are you blind, or something? It didn't seem . . .' She
broke off, seeing instantly the error of her words, damning
her naïvety in such matters. 'How silly of me.' She laughed
then, if only to show Alex that she was capable of laughing at herself. 'You *are* lovers!'

'Indeed?' Alex's eyebrows rose, but in such a way that
he neither affirmed nor denied Gina's assumption. 'We
used to be good friends, before she was married——'

'Married?' The information threw Gina completely.
How could Mandy consider herself a likely wife for Alex
if she was already married?

'She was divorced nine months ago. She's back living
with her parents now, so once again she's my neighbour,
like she told you.' He started the car and gave her a sideways look. 'I entertain quite frequently in Nairobi.
Mandy's been good enough to act as my hostess from
time to time. She makes a damn good job of it, too.'

He was silent for a moment before looking at her
thoughtfully. 'I see you've made one of your instant decisions.'

'What do you mean?'

'Well, you sat scowling at Mandy for the past hour. My
God, you're so intense, Gina! You took to Mandy the way
you've taken to Stella—with instant, irrational dislike!'

They were already approaching the *shamba* when Gina
replied to that. 'I don't like women who exploit them-
selves, that's all.'

'What's that supposed to mean?'

'Women who use . . . women who flirt outrageously!'

Alex was still laughing at her when he brought the car to a halt. Furious, Gina stumbled indoors and groped for the light switch. Just as she found it, Alex's hand closed around her wrist. 'What's wrong with a little flirting?'

'Let go of me!' Her back was against the wall as he towered over her, putting out an arm on either side of her, blocking her path.

'You should try it some time,' he smiled, 'you might discover things about yourself . . .'

'Are you so shallow that you judge all women by the clothes they wear, the way they look, their ability to flutter their eyelashes and flirt? Don't you ever look deeper, for the person rather than the image?'

He shrugged. 'Okay, I'll admit that Mandy comes on a little strong, but don't put her down for being herself.'

'You put me down for the same reason! And you haven't answered my question.'

'All right.' He was no longer smiling. 'If you want a serious answer, I'll give you one. I enjoy beauty. I like to see a woman make the most of herself, but of course I don't judge all women solely by appearance. Take Stella, for example, she'd still manage to be a lovely, elegant woman if she wore a sack. And Mandy, she'd still be a sex kitten if she dressed in a boiler suit. And they could achieve that because they are each fundamentally confident of what they are. Whereas you—you reflect an entirely false image. Tonight has made some improvement, I might add, but it's your——'

'Rubbish!' Gina hissed, wishing he would move away from her so she could think straight. 'I'm a student from twentieth-century England, Alex, I wish you'd get that through your head and stop being so old-fashioned. People dress——'

'People normally dress to reflect their personalities. But in your case it's a disguise. It's like a uniform, an image to hide behind because you're not confident of what and who you are. You're young, and I understand it, but——'

'Don't patronise me, for God's sake!' Tears were threateningly close, because once more his words struck a chord. She didn't need him to remind her that she'd been floating aimlessly through life for the past twelve months.

'I'm not simply talking about clothes, Gina, don't you see that? I'm talking about your whole attitude, your pugnaciousness, your aggression.'

'Alex, why are you always putting me down? You're the aggressor, not I!' Her lips trembled and she steeled herself not to cry—because she cared what he thought, when she shouldn't give a damn!

'Gina . . .' the sudden tenderness in his voice only made things worse, 'I'm trying to tell you to be yourself. Those funny modern ideas about what a woman should be are not your own. You're hiding behind them just as you hide behind your aggression. There's a switch inside you that hasn't yet been turned on . . .'

'Oh, really!' Her voice was as scathing as she could make it. 'This is becoming ridiculous!'

His only reply was his kiss. Gentle hands, firm hands, closed around her shoulders, leaving no escape from a kiss that persuaded her lips to part beneath his, until her mind reeled in confusion. But her body was not at all confused, it responded naturally, eagerly, to the slow caress of his hands as they moved sensuously from her shoulders, down the curve of her back to her hips.

But something was not right. Although she couldn't bring herself to pull away, Gina was aware of Alex's detachment. He was holding her yet keeping her away, kissing her yet somehow . . . almost punishing her! *Is* it some sort of punishment? she asked herself confusedly as he moved away from her. Was he just trying to prove a point?

'Well, I think I can discount my supposition that you have a basic contempt of men!' His smile was triumphant.

So he had been trying to prove a point!

Humiliated, angered, she cast around for a suitable response, but Alex just went on talking. 'Now don't get angry again. All I'm asking is that you be yourself, Gina. Relax, *give* of yourself.'

'I—wh-what do you mean?'

Her perplexity made him smile. 'Don't misunderstand me, dear girl, I don't mean physically. You should realise by now that you're safe with me. I was asked to look after you while you're here, so I'm not likely to take advantage of you, am I?'

Gina flushed stupidly. The thought hadn't entered her head! Oh, she just didn't understand him at all—any of this! But when she tried to move away his arms went around her again, holding her loosely yet captive within their circle. 'Alex, please, why are you doing this—let me go!'

'Listen to me.' His voice was a command, his deep blue eyes compelling her to look up at him. 'Listen to me, Gina Duncan, and I'll tell you what you are.'

She didn't want to hear any more! But there was no escape from him and though she tried hard mentally to block out his words, each and every one of them hit target.

'You're a girl with an enchanting smile, a smile which lights up your face and turns those big brown eyes into sparkling jewels. But, Gina, you smile so very, very rarely ... You're a girl with an innate sense of humour, but you're unable to laugh at life because you're so busy attacking it, and what it does to you. You're a girl with a svelte and beautiful body—but you hide it from the world not only with your clothes but in the way you move, the way you sit, the way you stalk about this house with a restlessness and ... sort of repressed anger ... that sets my teeth on edge.

'And that, in case you've wondered, is what I meant when I said you hide your light. Let it shine!' He laughed then, as if to lighten the mood, but Gina could only stare at him blankly. 'Somewhere behind all those masks is the delightful girl Harry once told me about. All you need is for someone to tell you you're a beautiful person, and you will *be* a beautiful person. Let's start all over again, shall we?'

He tilted her chin up, forcing her to bring her eyes back to his. 'I've attacked you ruthlessly, I know, but I did it for the best reasons, believe me. Give me another chance. Be beautiful for me!'

Be beaut——? What should she say? What could she say to a barrage of combined compliments and insults? Was he the most intuitive man she had ever met—or was he crazy? Was he right in all he had said—or was he wrong? Was he merely trying to win her over to his way of thinking, for peace's sake, for some unimaginable ulterior reason—or was he *right* about her?

Give him another chance? Regardless of their differences, surely he was giving *her* another chance ... hadn't she been the worst, most miserable guest one could be stuck with? Hadn't he, in fact, given her a dozen offers of starting afresh with all his invitations to have fun with him, to teach her things? And the first time she went out with him she had insulted his neighbour and ended the evening with the mammoth row she had known would be inevitable!

'Say something, Gina.' He threw back his head and laughed. 'Don't look so confused!'

'I—Alex ... I'll—yes——'

'You'll come out with me tomorrow? And the next day? Shall we enjoy this holiday *together*?'

'I—yes. Yes!' And then she was laughing, too. Laughing as he scooped her up in his arms and twirled her around, laughing as she hadn't laughed in a long, long time.

The storm started a little after four a.m. With a deafening crack of thunder it announced itself and shook Gina out of a sleep that had come astonishingly easily. Without hesitation she slipped out of bed, into a cotton nightie which had until now been redundant, and padded silently along the verandah just as the rain dropped from the skies like a solid sheet.

The experience which followed was one she would never forget. As fork after fork of lightning zig-zagged its way across the sky, the thunder rumbled and growled and the entire heavens were lit with a rich abundance of flowing colours that no artist on earth could capture. Stark, shocking, luminous reds, violets, yellows and blues shimmered across the sky in a tropical storm the likes of which she had read about but never actually witnessed. It was marvellous, like a gigantic painting in the making.

Without fear, without thought, Gina stepped outside, revelling in the cool, most welcome rain which brought with it a drop in temperature that could only be described as luxurious. Beyond the noise of the torrent there was silence, the inaudible sigh of the earth as it drank in that which it had been waiting for. Beneath the violence of the skies, there was peace.

Gina felt it, too. Inasmuch as this holiday would no longer be a torment, she was peaceful. She had made a fresh start with Alex. And while they could never be of one mind on many basic issues, at least there was no more fighting to be done. He wasn't here, now, to influence her with his nearness, to sway her with his reasoning. But he had convinced her of some things, her pugnaciousness and defensiveness not least. Maybe she was beautiful, maybe she was not. Did it really matter? Alex saw her only as a girl, a confused girl whom he kissed as a reward, or punishment—well, for any reason but the right one. He'd never kissed her because he wanted to. But that didn't matter, either. He would, of that she was sure. The challenge had become stronger than ever despite—or maybe because of—his compliments.

With the impetuosity of youth Gina sauntered over to the swimming pool and sat on the edge, her feet dangling in the water, leaning back on her hands as she flung back her head and smiled up at nature's angry display in the sky. She felt lonely then, but not unhappy. For the next two weeks, at least, she knew what life held in store for her. Tomorrow Alex would no longer be an adversary, but a friend. She would be beautiful for him . . . as far as she was able to be.

For a little while longer she sat there in a rain-soaked nightie, oblivious to the chill, oblivious of the dark outline of the man who stood behind the shutters of his bedroom. Watching her. Smiling at her. Understanding her . . . not wholly, but a great deal more than she understood herself.

CHAPTER FOUR

It was two days later when the letter came from her father. It was brief, saying simply that Uncle Ralph was making slow but steady progress and that Harry and Stella would be home within a few days. They would telephone and give an exact time of arrival.

Gina read the letter with mixed feelings. She was relieved about her uncle, of course, but the imminence of her father's return was a reminder of the reasons she had come to Africa, and how much sorting out she had yet to do about her future. In a way, she wanted to postpone her discussion with Harry; she was having so much fun with Alex that she wanted this holiday to go on and on. She could extend her holiday, of course, since she had no commitments now she had dropped out of school, no commitments at all . . . But no, she couldn't put off for ever the decisions that had to be made. Besides, things would be different when Stella and Harry got back.

On her return to the bungalow Lanu told her in his best broken English that Bwana had gone to check on the builders at her father's house. Gina went there in the car. It was a two-mile walk along the beach and she thought Alex might be glad of a lift home. Staying out in the sun for long stretches at a time didn't bother Alex, of course, although it was in fact cooler now the rains had started. So much cooler that Gini could tolerate the morning sun, at least.

Already she was able to water-ski. She had had two early morning sessions with Alex, one on the nearby creek and one on the ocean. It had been surprisingly easy— once she had got through her head that she mustn't bend her arms. Inevitably she had fallen off the skis, but Alex had been infinetely patient, standing behind her, holding her firmly until she gained her balance—then yelling instructions at her as Lanu sped the boat away and sent her hurtling through the crystal waters at a terrific pace.

They had crammed a lot into two days. Mandy Miller had called round twice to the bungalow, on different pretexts, but she hadn't managed to lure Alex away from Gina. Alex had shown Gina the ruins at Gedi, taken her to see the fascinating spectacle of the Wakamba Dancers; they had lunched at the beautiful Sindbad Hotel on the outskirts of Malindi, where they had eaten avocados and a delicious dish of game fish which Gina had later learned was wahoo cooked in coconut milk.

Tomorrow they would venture into Tsavo National Park, and the day after they planned to drive the seventy-five miles to Mombasa where, Alex had promised, they would go to his favourite restaurant and have the best seafood she had ever tasted.

With a guilty little smile Gina found herself hoping her father would be away for at least three more days . . .

'*Jambo!*' Alex called down to her from the top of a ladder perched against the side of her father's house.

'*Jambo! Habari!*' Gina answered him with the only two words of Swahili she'd so far mastered. 'Gosh, they're really going to town with this house, aren't they?'

'Well, it's their permanent resisdence, so they want to make the most of it.' Alex jumped the last few rungs and came to stand beside her, his arm going casually around her waist. 'What've you got there?'

'What does it look like?' she giggled, holding out at arm's length the two fresh lobsters she had bought from the young African who called daily at the beach houses, selling his catch.

Alex grinned at her. 'Are you trying to entice me home for lunch?'

'No. These are for dinner.'

'Can't be. Botana's got the evening off, I told you.'

'I'm cooking them.' She pulled a face at him, waiting for his retort.

'But surely you can't even cook an egg?' Even the sky was pale against the depth of the blue eyes that laughed down at her.

'I did learn some things in school, you know. Useful things!' She was able, now, to laugh with him, to take his teasing without getting angry. But she still gave as good as she got. 'I'll show you a thing or two, Alexander insolent Craig!'

She did, too. When evening came and Alex sat back in his chair, satisfied and replete, he was lavish with his praise. 'Gina, that was absolutely superb. Thank you. What was in that sauce, it was delicious?'

'Secret recipe.' She winked mischievously. 'So you see, finishing school does have its merits.'

'I take back everything I said about it!'

As Alex lit a cigarette Gina poured the *kahawa*, the delicious Kenyan coffee that was such a perfect finish for any meal. 'We did a Cordon Bleu course in school,' she shrugged, 'but to tell you the truth, cooking's always come easily to me. I practise my new dishes on my flatmates! It's not that they're incapable,' she hastened to add, 'it's just that they don't like cooking.'

'More Women's Libbers?' Alex raised an enquiring brow. 'Or is this Charles person one of your flatmates?'

'Charles? Good heavens, no!' The idea of sharing a flat with Charles was a joke. Charles . . . she hadn't even thought about him for days. In fact she hadn't thought about home, about London, at all. Being here was like living on a different planet, she couldn't envisage the hustle and bustle of London, the impure air, the shattering pace of life.

'It was a reasonable assumption,' Alex smiled. 'Lots of people share flats with the opposite sex in London. And it needn't imply——'

'Charles lives in a mansion!' she said forcefully, still laughing at the idea of him sharing a flat with herself and two girl friends. 'His stables are bigger than our flat—at least, his family's stables. He still lives with his parents. He'd die of claustrophobia living in our place!'

'Then what is he? Just a friend?'

'A boy-friend,' she conceded. 'Sort of.'

'I see.' There was a curious note in his voice. What was it . . . surprise, or what?

'As a matter of fact, he's a would-be husband.'

Alex's eyebrows shot up and he looked at her in mock horror. 'You don't say! Well, I hope you've straightened him out on a few things!'

'Indeed I have——' Her sentence was interrupted by the shrill ringing of the telephone. It was a curious sound, not at all like the phones at home. It was even more curious because it was the first time it had shown signs of life in a whole week.

'I'll get it.' As Gina headed for the phone it occurred to her that her father's letter had taken three days to get to Malindi; maybe he was ringing to say he'd be home to-morrow . . .

'Mr——? I'm sorry, what name was it? Ngara? Mr Ngara. Well, I'm sorry, but Mr Duncan isn't here at the moment.'

Alex walked over to her. 'I'll take it.'

'He's asking for Daddy.'

'Hand it over. I'll take a message.'

Alex took hold of the receiver and was immediately engrossed in a conversation spoken in Swahili. Gina went back to her coffee, watching him as he stood with his back to her. All she could decipher from the call was the mention of Nairobi. That, and the occasional curse in English as Alex moaned about the crackling on the lines.

When he joined her again, she saw that his mind was still on Mr Ngara's phone call. 'Is anything wrong?'

'Not at all.' He brightened instantly. 'Do you play chess? How about a game?'

'Certainly, but you'll have to teach me first.' She smiled to herself; chess was something she was very good at. She let Alex go through thirty minutes of explanation about the rudiments of the game, until he seemed fairly satisfied she knew enough to try her hand.

Forty minutes later, she had him in check. Alex looked at her in astonishment, his eyes going from the board to her impassive face, then back to the board. 'You little rogue!' She had him, he knew it, she knew it.

When she called checkmate she flopped back on the settee and laughed her head off.

Alex helped himself to a Scotch from the bar, cursing her, cursing himself because it was the second time she'd fooled him. But his laughter soon died away and as he sat down beside her, his next words took her by surprise.

'Gina, I have to go to Nairobi tomorrow.'

Hiding her disappointment came easily to Gina; she'd had lots of practice. 'Is it something to do with that phone call?'

There was the slightest hesitation before he answered. 'I have some business to attend to. Will you come with me?'

The thought of another journey so soon in one of those rickety planes—with possible turbulence—held no attraction whatsoever. And she told him. She told him all about her journey down from Nairobi a week ago.

It was something Alex was obviously used to. He sympathised about it, but shrugged off her reticence with further news. 'I have my own plane. It's at the aerodrome just a few miles from here. If we hit turbulence, I'll simply drop her altitude,' he said, speaking of his plane as if it were a person. 'Come to think of it, that'd be more interesting for you. I'll fly her reasonably low so you can get a good look at everything. Come with me, Gina, and I'll be your guide! And in the evening I'll wine you and dine you, and we'll dance. Bear in mind, however, that if you tell me you can't dance, I'm just not going to believe it!' He looked down meaningfully at the chessboard.

Alex was as good as his word. There was no fear in Gina as they sailed beneath a perfectly blue sky in the very early hours the following morning in a six-seater plane Alex fondly referred to as 'Mitzi'. He handled his plane as well as he handled his car, fully in command, as always.

Gina saw far more of the Tsavo National Park than she could ever have seen in a day's outing by car. She was fascinated, growing fonder of Kenya by the minute as she watched through Alex's binoculars the spritely movement of gazelles, the eland, zebra and a whole host of animals who made their homes in the bush. She was even lucky enough to see a herd of elephants.

Alex chatted to her all the way. It seemed that once he got talking about his country, he couldn't stop. Gina turned to watch him, fascinated as much by the look in his eyes as she was by his narrative. There was no doubt that Alex Craig loved his country very much.

'I'm sure you'll like my home. It's about seven miles outside Nairobi, set high on a hill and overlooking acres and acres of coffee.' His ready smile made Gina's stomach contract slightly. 'That's what I do, you know—I'm a plantationer.'

'Among other things?' She was thinking of what Mandy Miller had told her about Alex's expenditure on a drinks factory.

But Alex didn't mention that. He merely shrugged. 'First and foremost I'm a man of the land. It's in my blood.'

'Where did your family originate?' Gina was interested to know more. This was the first time Alex had volunteered anything about himself.

'My great-grandfather was English, his wife Scottish. They came here pretty late in life, started with just a few acres of land. My grandfather took over, then my father, and despite a very difficult time politically, my father, my brother and I went——'

'Your brother? Does he live with you?' Gina was instantly sorry she'd interrupted him, because he suddenly clammed up.

'He's dead,' he replied curtly. 'My parents, too.'

She wanted to ask him about it, but couldn't bring herself to. Alex's face was set, unsmiling, and he was suddenly concentrating on his flying far more than he had been before.

When he brought the plane to a halt after a perfectly smooth landing, however, he was himself again. That was something Gina liked about Alex, his anger or his moods were very shortlived. He was quickly back on an even keel, relaxed, smiling and with that air of optimism and total self-assurance.

'Okay! Now to practical matters. I've got a car waiting here, Gina. You have the choice of waiting for me at the house or doing a solo sightseeing trip round the city. What will it be? I'm afraid I'll be gone most of the day, but I'll join you between three and four this afternoon.'

'I'm going shopping,' she said positively. She knew precisely what she was going to do with her day. Her time alone with Alex was limited—and that challenge still beckoned very strongly . . .

'Right!' He fished in his pocket and handed her some money, eyeing her white shorts and sun-top rather doubtfully. 'Buy yourself a dress, then. I don't think that outfit will go down very well where I'm taking you tonight.'

'I will.' Her voice was haughty as he looked down at the money he was offering. 'And I have money, thank you.'

He grinned at her. 'All right, little Miss Independent. Be beautiful for me!'

Oh, she intended to!

Alex dropped her off in the city centre. A light drizzle

was in the air, but that didn't bother her. It was a nice balance between the bursts of torrential rain which were now pervading the coast, and the heat she had suffered prior to it. It was generally cooler in Nairobi, too, thanks to the fact that it was thousands of feet above sea-level.

The day sped by very pleasantly. It was good to be in a city again. Nairobi was small compared to London, but huge compared to Malindi. Gina traipsed around from shop to shop and ended up with only one carrier-bag. But it contained everything she would need for the evening.

Her final call was at the hairdressers. It was sheer luxury to have a scalp massage and lashings of sweet-smelling conditioner which put back a glorious blue-black shine on hair that had taken something of a beating down on the coast.

It was exactly three o'clock when she got to her designated meeting place, the pavement café outside the Thorntree. Gina sat underneath the massive tree from which the restaurant took its name, ordered a beer and sat for forty minutes absolutely fascinated by the comings and goings of the customers. There were people from all walks of life, all the countries of the world, it seemed. Rich and poor alike, indigenous people and visiting jet-setters; the turnover of customers was astonishing in a spot which was obviously a very popular meeting place.

Although Alex was smiling broadly when he joined her, Gina knew at once that something was wrong. She didn't pry, she didn't comment, but she had grown very adept at reading his eyes and knew that all was not well with him. He hid it well, whatever it was, and within minutes he had Gina chatting to him, telling him about the people she had been watching.

She fell in love with Alex's house immediately it came into view. Set on a hill, it was built from brick and wood on three storeys. Around the entire house, on the ground and first floors, there was a wide verandah; it was old, large and rambling, sitting comfortably among acres and acres of coffee bushes planted neatly across land which had been formed into platforms, steps, so the best advantage could be gained from the rains.

The interior of the house was bright and airy, the walls painted white, the floors wooden, polished meticulously. The furnishings were old but well cared for and very comfortable. It was very much a masculine sort of house, the occasional rugs, paintings and sculptures lending a light relief.

Around the house were massive gardens abundant with exotic trees and flowers. The palm trees surrounding the swimming pool area provided a privacy which was uncalled for. One could not be overlooked here except, perhaps, by the Ngong Hills whose graceful slopes were visible in the distance. The view was breathtaking in its beauty.

After having tea by the pool, served to them by Alex's old and trusty servant, a tall, thin Kikuyu named Kimau, Gina retired to a guest room on the first floor and slept away the rest of the afternoon.

Her dress was white, made from fine Indian cotton. Skimpy little shoulder-straps led to a bodice which was covered with layers of narrow, delicate lace finishing at the waist where it fitted Gina's slender figure to perfection. The skirt was plain, lending a little more width to her hips because it was quite full, knee-length. She had bought a tiny white leather bag and very high-heeled sandals to match. The dress was still on a hanger, the sandals and bag on the bed, waiting for her to add the finishing touches to her make-up before she put them on.

Although she didn't ordinarily wear make-up, Gina knew what suited her. She had experimented with it often—something else finishing school could be thanked for. She was subtle with it, just a touch of shading around eyes which were already large, and a single layer of mascara on lashes which were already black and enviably long. Her skin needed no enhancing, her complexion was smooth and clear, glowing with the gentle tan she had quickly acquired after being exposed to the African sun for a few days.

On her lips she put a pale pink gloss which matched exactly the nail varnish she had bought. The tiny pink earrings she had found complemented her dark hair and she took trouble brushing it into a shining cloud around her face.

It wasn't until she'd finished her preparations with a few dabs of expensive French perfume that Gina took a long, hard look at herself in the mirror. No, she wasn't being false to herself in taking all this trouble, she had enjoyed doing it. It was a startling thought. Never before had she gone to such lengths in order to look her best. But then never before had she had such an incentive. She wanted to please Alex, and if this was pandering to a man, then so be it. The surprising thing was that in wanting to please him, she was also pleasing herself. She *liked* the way she looked tonight.

Her courage deserted her after she had dressed. She looked so—so young. Was the dress just too unsophisticated, even little-girlish? What would he think of it? Would it be right for the restaurant? In a sudden spasm of nervousness Gina walked slowly downstairs, unable to delay any longer and knowing that if Alex criticised her or teased her in any way, it would ruin her plans completely.

He was in the lounge, standing by the open glass doors which overlooked the magnificent view of his land, motionless, unaware that he was being watched from the door to the interior of the house. Dressed in a white dinner jacket with a crisp white shirt, black bow-tie and trousers, he looked superb. He looked, he was, everything Gina was not . . . sophisticated, controlled, totally self-confident. But then he had looked that way before she had got to know him, when he was wearing nothing more than a loin-cloth and driving a tatty old Land Rover.

As her eyes travelled to his beautiful profile, Gina's heart contracted slightly, a sensation which was immediately followed by a sense of disappointment. He was still worried about something, far away in his thoughts. Whatever had happened at his business meeting today still continued to trouble him. Gina was at a loss to understand it; hadn't they come to Nairobi as a result of Mr Ngara's phone call? But Mr Ngara had wanted to speak to Harry . . .

But as Alex turned and saw her, all other thoughts were chased from her mind. He was smiling, his eyes lit with approval and a surprise which shattered his reverie and left him concentrating solely on her.

'Gina! Is it you? My, my, is this the same girl I once met at Malindi airport?' She laughed softly as she reached for his outstretched hand and stood with butterflies chasing round her stomach as he looked her over from head to toe.

Thanks to the high heels she was taller, but she still had to look up to him. From beneath her lowered lashes she smiled at him shyly, trying her best to be casual. 'You look beautiful! You *are* beautiful!' His arm went easily, comfortably around her waist as he drew her towards him.

They stood quietly, looking out over the shadowy outline of the hills, enjoying a silence which was almost tangible. 'You were right, Alex, I do like your home. Your land, the view—it's incredibly peaceful and lovely here.'

He nodded, smiling, a strange note in his voice as he acknowledged her praise. 'And even more so when there's a beautiful woman by my side to appreciate it with me . . . What will you have to drink, Gina? It's a little too early to leave just yet.'

From a perfect beginning there followed the most wonderful evening of Gina's life. In a white, open-topped sports car they drove through Nairobi to the outskirts of the city. At the doorway of the nightclub a uniformed African greeted Alex by name, smiling that familiar Kenyan smile as he took the keys and drove the car to the car park. They were greeted like royalty by the manager of the club and the head waiter led them to their table, saying something about Alex's 'usual table' having been reserved for him.

The club was gorgeous, a circular room which was small enough to lend an air of intimacy. Facing the entrance there was a small stage and a dance-floor. The front of the bar was covered in zebra-skin, the jackets of the waiters made from black and white material reminiscent of a similar thing. The inner circle of tables, already fully occupied by people who were drinking but not eating, were drums covered with glass tops. Everywhere there were exotic plants and flowers, and let into one wall was a huge aquarium which housed colourful little fish of all sizes and shapes, swimming lazily in the dimly-lit water.

Alex and Gina were seated in a semi-circular booth against the far wall which gave them a clear view of the stage. The lighting, the seating, the soft music and friendly smiles combined to make a perfect atmosphere in which Gina was entirely relaxed. Her dress was perhaps not quite right; there were some women present who had dressed to the nines in slinky, full-length dresses complete with plentiful and expensive jewellery. But if Gina looked only her nineteen years and unsophisticated, Alex didn't seem to mind. He was the essence of charm and wonderfully attentive to her.

Their surroundings, in fact, became almost irrelevant once they resumed their chatting. All through dinner they talked while others danced to the music of a combo whose repertoire seemed designed to please every taste.

Ridiculously, incongruously, they talked politics. They talked art. They talked about England where, Gina discovered, Alex had spent four years at school. Over and over again he surprised her; with his knowledge, his reasoning, and—yes, with a sensitivity she once would never have given him credit for.

It was when they talked about the music of Beethoven that Alex became totally engrossed, delighted, fascinated by Gina's knowledge and envious of the concerts she had been to in London. It was with something approaching resentment that they responded to the start of the cabaret—it meant they had to stop talking. Never in her life had Gina met anyone remotely like Alex Craig. He was, she acknowledged, everything she wanted and respected in a man.

When the cabaret was over and the soft music resumed, Alex grinned at her and reached for her hand. 'If we don't have at least one dance, I shall consider this evening incomplete. Do you realise that we might just as well have dined at home this evening and entertained ourselves?'

She agreed with him, her laughter tinkling as he led her to the dance floor and took her in his arms. It was then that it happened. As the full length of their bodies pressed close, the atmosphere between them became electric. The shock of excitement, the physical awareness, the beginnings of arousal were not new to Gina. Alex had made her feel like this before, when he had kissed her, when he touched her even casually. The difference was that tonight, now, he was feeling it, too.

When he moved away from her slightly, Gina was not perturbed. So, once again they were intimately close, and once again Alex was holding her at bay! But it wouldn't work. Not tonight! Tonight there would be no barriers, no detachment on his part. Tonight his kiss would not be that of a friend, nor that of a tormentor . . .

The expression in his eyes was intense, unfamiliar; he seemed to be looking deep inside her, as if he had never really seen her before. But then he had not. She'd never been like this before. Beautiful, a perfect companion, charming, witty, and growing more confident by the minute. The challenge was half met; she was affecting Alex Craig and she knew it. But it was not enough. Not yet!

She moved closer to him, aware that the increasing number of dancers was giving her the perfect excuse to close the gap between them. 'Gina . . .' She felt the tension in him as his arms tightened around her, their bodies moving in precise harmony, to the music, to each other.

She said nothing. She was too close to look at him now. With a gentle, natural movement she leaned her cheek against his shoulder, her breasts pressing against the hardness of his chest, not stopping to think that she might be playing with fire. The feel of him, the beating of his heart, the warmth of his body, the smell of freshly laundered linen and the faintest whiff of after-shave combined to intoxicate her, body and mind. But not once did it occur to her that she might lose control, that when she had finally got Alex Craig where she wanted him, her little game would backfire on her.

'I—think we'd better call it a day.' The low tones of Alex's deep voice broke the spell and she smiled up at him lazily.

'Not yet, Alex . . .'

'We're making an early start back to Malindi tomorrow.' His voice was tinged with a harshness she couldn't understand. 'Besides, it's getting very crowded in here.'

The car was waiting for them as they left. Alex drove just one hundred yards down the road in an atmosphere which was so charged between them it was almost like a physical presence. Gina smiled to herself as he brought the car to an abrupt halt, knowing what he was about to do and revelling in a feeling of triumph as he pulled her roughly into his arms.

Her lips were parted, moist, meeting his own with a need and a hunger which startled her. But it was all too brief, leaving her wanting more and more . . .

'You little witch!' Alex's voice was low, rough, tinged

with surprise. 'You've held me spellbound all evening
until I can hardly resist you. I have to hand it to you,
Gina, when you learn—you learn fast!'

Her laugh was mischievous, delighted. She'd heard
what she wanted to hear—but still something was driving
her on. She wanted more of this, much more. They drove
home in a silence which spoke volumes, yet left so much
unsaid. The electric, physical attraction hung in the air
between them like an uninvited guest, preventing them
from talking while at the same time it rendered any form
of conversation unnecessary.

Gina was shattered when Alex bade her goodnight
immediately they stepped indoors, virtually ordering her
to bed as if she were a child who had stayed out too long!

'I—why so abrupt, Alex? Let's have a nightcap, at
least.' When he hesitated, she urged him on. 'I can't
possibly sleep just yet.' She gave him her sweetest smile,
linking her arm through his. 'Come on, I'm far too high
from a beautiful evening. Let's wind down over a drink.'

He agreed reluctantly, leaving her to ponder over his
sudden change of mood. As he was pouring two glasses of
brandy she went over to the bar, standing close to him,
looking up at him appealingly. 'Alex, have I said something to upset you? I mean, didn't you have a nice evening?'

'Fabulous. It was the best evening I've had in a long
time, Gina. You're quite a girl, you know.'

'Then why did you want to end it so abruptly?'

His smile was wry. 'Dear girl, if you need to ask me
such a question then you must be even more innocent
than I take you for. Don't you realise the effect you're
having on me tonight?'

Of course she realised. She wasn't that innocent. But
perhaps it was that which was putting him off now. Maybe
he preferred a more experienced woman—like Mandy
Miller, for instance.

Gina pursed her lips, smiling mysteriously, getting in

deeper and deeper by the minute. 'I'm not the innocent you take me for, Alex. You've jumped to so many conclusions about me—wrong conclusions.' She slipped her arms around his neck, her fingers twining in the little curls at the base of his hair, inviting his kiss with her every movement.

She could feel the tension inside him, that damned restraint he was exercising again. 'Don't take on more than you can handle, Gina. I'm not a teenager who'll be satisfied with a few kisses . . .'

'Let me worry about what you need,' she murmured, her body pressing tightly against his. 'I told you, I haven't been living in a nunnery.'

He kissed her then, hard and long. He kissed her because he could no longer resist it. Soon she'd have won! Soon she would show Alex Craig she was every ounce a woman. Then she would stop, switch off. And she would tell him to eat his words . . . when she held the same power over him as he held over her right now.

But it all went wrong, terribly wrong. It was a hollow victory indeed, for when the challenge was met there was no turning back, no stopping. She had disregarded his warning, and now it was impossible not to respond. Alex was kissing her as he had never kissed her before, hungrily, passionately, his lips probing and demanding a response she gave willingly, involuntarily.

She was weak with longing, her entire body consumed with a need she hadn't realised existed. His mouth moved hungrily across her face, her throat, as his fingers pulled the dress straps from her shoulders. His hands covered her breasts, caressing slowly, rhythmically, taking her nipples between her fingers in the most erotic, tantalising fashion.

When his mouth sought her breasts and his lips closed over the firm, sensitive flesh of her nipples a cry escaped from her, her body arching against him in invitation, a plea for the only thing that would satisfy the need he had awoken in her.

But Alex drew away, his fingers biting into her shoulders as he pushed her from him, his eyes half closed, his voice ragged as he fought for control. 'Gina, this is insane!'

'Alex, please!' she cried, not wanting to listen, knowing only that she wanted, needed his loving. Her arms went around him, her fingernails trailing lightly down his back until her hands reached his hips and she pulled him tightly against her, pushing her own body against him wantonly.

'For God's sake, Gina, I'm thinking of Harry,' he said thickly, his voice so drenched with arousal that she could barely hear him. Again he was looking at her as if he had never seen her before. 'Maybe you do have the morals of a tomcat, but your father thinks you sweet and innocent, and he certainly didn't have this in mind when he asked me to look after you!'

But Gina was like one possessed. She wasn't thinking of principles, Alex Craig's—or her own! She was thinking of nothing but this moment, of Alex's nearness, of the hungry ache inside her. Her hand moved from his hip, sliding between their bodies until she was touching him very intimately, absolutely shamelessly.

With a low, animal groan Alex locked his arms around her, his lips crushing hers in a passion that was no longer controllable. Whether she had won—or lost—did not occur to her then. She was incapable of thought, incapable of anything but a wild response to Alex Craig's lovemaking. She didn't even hear the knock on the door. It was only when Alex released her with a violent curse that she became aware of the interruption.

The next few moments passed in a blur. Alex was standing by the door, holding it ajar and talking to his manservant in a language she didn't understand. Gina was fighting to regain her equilibrium, her sanity, straightening her clothes, reaching for the untouched brandy on the bar. She was trembling from head to toe when he came back to her, suddenly embarrassed and incredulous that she had behaved the way she had.

'I'm sorry about that. It seems that Kimau had waited up especially to give us a message.' Alex reached for the other drink and swallowed it in one go.

'Why the hell didn't he leave you a note?' She didn't mean to snap, and even as she was filled with an irrational resentment of Kimau, she knew she should be grateful to him.

'Because he can neither read nor write,' Alex said simply. 'Stella phoned. The call came through about an hour ago, it seems. They'd been trying to reach us at the coast. She and your father are halfway home, Gina, they'll arrive at Malindi airport around five tomorrow afternoon.'

'I . . . see.' She didn't know what else to say.

'I'm afraid that's not all of it. Your Uncle Ralph died three days ago and your father's unwell. He's taken it very badly.'

CHAPTER FIVE

HAVING been told that her father was unwell did not prepare Gina for the reality of it. He looked drawn, thinner in face and in body. His bushy hair seemed to have a lot more grey in it than she remembered from their last meeting, and despite his suntan there was a greyness about his face that worried her instantly. In his dark brown eyes, eyes so much like her own, there was an incredible sadness that made her heart twist painfully as she looked at him.

In answer to her opening question Harry waved a dismissive arm and told his daughter he was fine, just fine. Gina hugged him gently, briefly, knowing full well how he was feeling, but appearing to accept his word. Like father, like daughter; Gina did not go in for long, emotional diatribes.

'You'll be just fine when you've had a rest, won't you, darling?' The smooth, female voice with a slight American accent spoke reassuringly, possessively.

'Hello, Stella.'

'Hello, Gina dear. Are you well? I'm so sorry we weren't here to greet you, but I know you've been in good hands with Alex.'

Alex smiled at her, reaching for her suitcases. There were two of them, needless to say. He summoned a porter to collect Harry's case and led the way to the car, Harry and Stella on either side of him.

Harry was subdued on the way back to the bungalow, sitting in the back of the car with his wife, leaving it to her to make the explanations. There wasn't much to say, really. Uncle Ralph had died after Harry had written to Gina. The funeral had taken place two days later.

'Good grief, Georgina,' Harry put in suddenly, as if

86

he'd only just realised, 'what's happened to your hair? It was down to your waist this time last year.'

'Was it, indeed?' Alex glanced over at her and raised a sardonic eyebrow. 'That must have been something to behold. Er—I think Gina's changed her image once or twice since you last saw her, Harry.'

'It's awful,' the older man said, as blunt as ever.

'Oh, I think it suits her,' Stella said lightly, a smile in her voice which Gina couldn't interpret. 'As a matter of fact, I was thinking how pretty you look today, Gina.'

'I like it.' Gina's voice was crisp, making it clear that she wasn't interested in Stella's opinion of her—appearance or anything else. She felt, rather than saw, Alex's annoyance as she kept her eyes on the road ahead.

Coming from Stella a remark like that was high praise indeed—or bitchiness in the extreme. *She* looked gorgeous, of course. She had stepped from the plane after a long and gruelling journey looking as if she had just posed for the front cover of some high-class women's magazine. She was wearing a pale lemon shift in pure silk, white accessories and a large-brimmed picture hat which very few women of her age would get away with. But then Stella didn't look anything like her thirty-eight years.

When they got indoors Gina's father sank his stocky frame into the nearest armchair, put his feet up and didn't even attempt to keep his eyes open.

'Harry darling, I think you'd be better in bed—have a proper sleep.' Stella crooned at him. Then, in a similar coaxing fashion, 'Alex, pet, would you fix me a large gin and tonic—just the way I like it!'

'With pleasure, my love.' Alex smiled indulgently as he immediately complied with Stella's request.

My love? Pet? What sort of sloppiness was this? Gina looked from one to the other in surprise. By the time her eyes travelled to her father's, the look had become one of distaste. But Harry didn't react at all. Gina assumed he had fallen asleep—until he told his wife he would like a cup of tea. Stella went immediately to the kitchen to convey the order to Botana. It was then that Alex asked what Gina would like to drink.

'Beer,' she said sullenly, resentful of the way Alex was treating Stella and considering Gina only as an after-thought. It had been the same in the car, the pair of them had chatted non-stop, bringing Gina into the conversation just as a matter of courtesy.

'Georgina, don't you think it's high time you progressed to something more—suitable—for a young lady?' Harry spoke to her without opening his eyes, his voice weary. 'I thought you'd have passed the beer-drinking stage by now.'

If Alex Craig even attempted to suppress his laughter, he didn't succeed. 'It sounds as though your daughter's been going through various phases and changes, eh, Harry?'

Gina glared at him furiously. He was laughing at her, just trying to reiterate a point he had made to her days ago—an eternity ago. Didn't he realise it was no longer necessary?'

'It's no laughing matter,' her father barked gruffly. 'I send her to the most expensive schools in the world, and she turns out like this!'

'Daddy, what on earth are you going on about?' Gina threw him a look of disgust which was entirely wasted. Harry Duncan didn't change. Illness or no illness, he was as down to earth as ever. Her father, that broad, gruff, bear of a man whom she adored. How infuriating he could be at times!

Harry condescended to open his eyes then. 'Madam, the last I heard of you was what I read in the news-papers—we do get newspapers here, you know. There was an article in it which stated that the daughter of Harry Duncan, retired store-owner, etcetera, etcetera, was seen in a fashionable London restaurant with a party of intoxi-cated females, one of whom stood on the table and removed her dress! What have you got to say about that? And I'd ask you to bear in mind that you are named as Harry Duncan's daughter, apart from anything else.'

Point taken, Gina lowered her gaze. 'Sorry about that. But it had nothing to do with me, Daddy. They were friends of one of my flatmates. I'd gone out with them because it was her birthday. I could hardly refuse the invitation. They are—a little wild.'

As she said the words she realised now what Harry had meant in his comment to Alex. So that was it! 'I don't mix with them ordinarily,' she assured her father, in awe of him despite the fact that she was almost a woman now.

'I'm glad to hear it.' Harry didn't seem at all convinced.

Stella came back then, glancing from one person to the next as if she could sense the tension in the air. 'Tea's on the way, Harry. And I've told Botana what to cook for dinner.'

It was quite the wrong thing to say. 'I'd already given him instructions,' Gina informed her.

'Oh!' Stella smoothed down her sleek chestnut hair, soft green eyes smiling graciously. 'Then I'll go and have another word with him, of course.'

'Leave it, Stella,' Gina said sharply. 'It doesn't matter. It doesn't matter in the least.'

Stella sat down, realising it would be best to leave it alone, and tactfully moving on to another subject so the moment's awkwardness would quickly pass.

From behind the bar Alex Craig appraised the younger woman coolly. His jaw was set, his mouth unsmiling, leaving her in no doubt that he was annoyed by the way she had spoken to her stepmother. That, and what else? What had he made of Harry's revelation about that scene in the restaurant? It mattered to her. She didn't want him thinking she ran around with the sort of girl who would take off her clothes in a public place. She didn't want him *really* to believe she had the morals of a tomcat. But why shouldn't he, when she'd seduced him shamelessly less than twenty-four hours ago!

Dinner that evening was a rather difficult affair for Gina.

Her father continued to be withdrawn, listless, picking at his food and eating very little of it. Come to think of it, the only time he had spoken to her since his return had been to criticise her. That, plus his demand for an explanation about the unfortunate newspaper article. Harry had always been strict. Even from a distance his personal code of conduct had held her in check over the years; she had always done what was expected of her. Until now . . .

Gina sighed inwardly. In his present mood, there was no way she was able to tell her father she had dropped out of art school. She would have to wait for a couple of days, until he was feeling better, until he began to get over his brother's death.

'You're very preoccupied, Gina dear.' Stella was smiling graciously from the other side of the table. 'I was asking you what you thought of our new house.'

Stella was expert at keeping a pleasant conversation going, smoothing over a difficult atmosphere. But then she'd had full co-operation from Alex, who had been hanging on to her every word, laughing at her witicisms and generally behaving as though she were royalty.

'It's fine,' Gina shrugged. 'Whatever turns you on. Personally I can't understand why you and Daddy want to live here permanently, although the coast is very nice for a holiday. I should have thought Nairobi a better choice, the shopping's better and there's more nightlife.'

If Gina's sarcasm struck home, Stella didn't show it. She smiled indulgently. 'My dear, Harry and I love it here. We're both at the stage now when we want as much peace as we can get. Isn't that right, darling?'

'It certainly is.' Harry patted his wife's hands affectionately, his adoration of her unmistakable in his eyes. There was a certain amount of adoration in Alex's eyes too—for Stella, not for Gina. Gina avoided looking at the man by her side. His nearness was affecting her, as ever, although tonight it had nothing to do with sex. Tonight Gina was filled with a different sort of tension. She was filled with a need to talk with Alex, in private. And yet . . . and yet she realised that she suddenly had nothing to say to him. Nothing at all.

Straight after dinner Harry excused himself and went to bed. He didn't even stay around for coffee. Stella looked at him anxiously, saying she would take care not to disturb him and would leave him to lie in in the morning. She was worried about him, that was obvious. So was Gina. Even Alex became rather tense after Harry's departure, although it was nothing Gina could put her finger on. She wondered what was on his mind. Concern for his friend—or something else?

When Gina announced that she was going out for a walk, Stella put down her coffee cup and looked at her anxiously. 'Gina, if you're worrying about your father, please don't. I'll be honest with you, his angina has been playing him up quite badly, and he's naturally upset about his brother. But he'll be all right now he's home. I know best how to handle it, believe me. After a few days' rest——'

'Yes, I know. I think I can read my father as well as you, Stella. But I'm sure you know best how to handle him. You are his wife, after all.'

'Yes, she is.' Alex's voice cracked across the room. He was standing behind the bar, pouring a liqueur for Stella. 'And I for one wish you would come to terms with that fact.'

'Alex darling, I'm sure Gina didn't mean——' Strangely enough, Stella jumped to Gina's defence, but Alex just talked over her.

'Here.' He threw the car keys across to Gina. 'Take the car and make it a drive instead. It'll be safer than walking through the *shamba* at this time of night.'

'Do—do you want to come, Alex?' It cost her a lot to ask him that, especially when she knew what the answer would be. She wanted to talk to him, she hoped he would realise it, but if he did he disregarded it.

'No, thank you.'

Gina left abruptly. Damn him! He was angry with her because of her attitude to Stella. Ye gods, she was entitled to her opinion, wasn't she? She simply didn't like the woman, and that was all there was to it!

She didn't take the car. Nor had she any intention of walking through the *shamba* where there might be all sorts of things crawling around. Instead she headed for the beach. Sitting by the water's edge would be safe enough—with only the big orange moon for company.

The task of sorting out her thoughts and feelings was not an easy one for Gina. Except for one thing. For his timely interruption last night, Gina would be eternally grateful to Alex's old and faithful servant. Last night she had wanted to make love with Alex Craig more than she had wanted anything else in her life. Now, in the cold light of reason, she saw that it would have been the wrong thing to do.

Despite her emancipation, the fact that she was young and modern, somewhere deep inside her she was basically old-fashioned in some respects. Probably due to her father's attitude and influence.

Had she gone to bed with Alex, she would have had difficulty looking her father in the face today. Alex would have felt that way, too—he had virtually said as much. It certainly explained his reluctance, and there was tremendous satisfaction in knowing his reluctance had been for that reason and not due to lack of attraction.

No, there was no lack in Gina now. Alex was as attracted to her physically as she was to him. Maybe he always had been, despite their initial, mutual dislike. Physical attraction very often made no sense at all. Alex liked her now, however. She was confident of that. But what of it—all of it? She had to face facts. At best their relationship had developed into a sort of holiday romance which was leading precisely nowhere. In fact, today had already put an end to it. Alex was so—different—today. And the presence of Harry and Stella would prohibit anything further from developing.

That thought pulled her up short. What on earth was she thinking about? She had to go home soon! She had almost forgotten why she came here! She didn't belong here, with Stella and Harry. The trouble was that she didn't really belong anywhere . . .

Art school hadn't been right for her, nor did she belong with her contemporaries, who bored her. Even the thought of Charles, who was six years older, made her exasperated now. Alex Craig had ruined any attraction there might have been there. Compared to Alex, Charles was boring in the extreme, with his horses, his toffee-nosed friends and constant round of dinner parties.

No, if she belonged anywhere it was with Alex Craig. He was sophisticated, intelligent, knowledgeable—and unpredictable. All of which excited her! Furthermore, she felt she had a lot to offer him, too. This, without even considering the overwhelming physical attraction between them. But what use was there in thinking along these lines?

Kicking off her sandals, Gina walked to the water's edge, letting the water lap around her ankles as she looked up at the moon, out across the vast expanse of the Indian Ocean. She was suddenly consumed by a choking sense of loneliness. She was falling in love with Alex Craig—why deny it any longer? The wisest thing to do was to get the hell out of Africa while she still had some control over her emotions. And in the meantime avoid any privacy with Alex so she could keep her traitorous body in check, too. She must talk to her father as soon as possible.

She picked up her sandals and walked across the beach, back to the bungalow. As she padded quietly up the steps she could hear the low tones of Alex's voice on her approach. What he said made her stop in her tracks. She stood stock still and listened, unable to imagine what he and Stella were talking about so fervently.

'. . . and how long do you think we can keep this thing quiet?' Alex was saying.

'For as long as I think fit,' Stella replied levelly. 'His health isn't the only consideration. I've told you, he's got some really Victorian ideas.' Then, her voice coaxing, 'Alex, let's leave everything as we've just discussed.'

There was a pause before Alex spoke again. 'All right. All things considered, I suppose you're being wise. We can't tell him.'

'Then you'll do it my way?'

'Of course,' Alex laughed then. 'You know I could never refuse you anything, my sweet.'

There followed an ominous silence—and then Stella's soft laughter.

A cold hand closed around Gina's heart. Were they . . . kissing? What on earth had they been talking about? What was it that they'd agreed not to tell Harry? It had to be Harry they were talking about—referring to his health and his Victorian ideas. What the devil was going on? An overwhelming nausea swept over Gina then. Surely there wasn't something between Alex and Stella? It couldn't be! It was just too—too awful to consider!

As much as she disliked her stepmother, Gina could not believe she would carry on behind her husband's back. Everything she did showed a concern for her husband— unless she was a damned good actress! And what of Alex? If his principles had prevented him from making love to his friend's daughter, surely he couldn't possibly have something going with his friend's wife!

Gina backed away quietly and escaped into her bedroom at the far end of the verandah, chiding herself, knowing that she must be mistaken. But it certainly didn't sound that way. There was something going on which Alex and Stella were keeping from Harry . . .

It kept her awake, especially when she thought of the blatant fondness in Alex's eyes whenever he looked at the older woman. And hadn't he sung her praises—talked about her being *all woman*—until Gina was sick of it?

It was some time later that Gina became aware there

was someone in her room. She had no idea of the time, and when she recognised the large, masculine frame approaching her bed in the darkness she shut her eyes tightly, feigning sleep.

There was a sharp dig in her shoulder and Alex's voice, harsh with annoyance. 'Gina, if you're asleep you can bloody well wake up and explain yourself!'

She stirred slowly, anger sweeping over her. 'What is it?'

'Why didn't you let us know you were back? We were worried sick about you. We saw the car . . . thought you'd been murdered or something!'

'Don't be so dramatic, Alex—I went for a walk.' She peered at him through the darkness, hating him as memories of the scene she had overheard came back to her, loving him as very different memories came into play.

'Well, you might have had the manners to let us know you'd come back into the house!'

Why was he so cross? For the reasons he was giving— or because he had been having a furtive conversation with Stella, and didn't know whether he had been overheard?

'I'm sorry,' she lied, wanting only to get rid of him.

He seemed quite satisfied with that. 'All right.' Then, 'But you had Stella really worried! I wish you'd remember your manners, Gina, and curb that vicious tongue of yours when you talk to her.'

There was no reply.

'I'm taking her skiing in the morning. Will you join us?'

'I should have thought Stella would consider water-skiing rather infra dig.'

'My God, you can be a bitch at times!' he snapped. 'I take it that means no?'

'You take it right.'

He left her then, stalking out of the room silently and leaving his anger hanging in the air behind him.

At three in the morning Gina found herself outside,

sitting once again under the moonlight by the swimming pool. The insomnia she'd begun to think she'd conquered was back with a vengeance.

'I'm a very lucky man,' Harry announced, quite out of the blue. He and Gina were sitting on the patio taking a late breakfast, and as Gina followed her father's gaze she saw that Stella and Alex had just come into view on the ocean in front of the bungalow.

'She really loves your old dad, you know. And she's just about the most wonderful woman in the world. Yes, I'm a very lucky man.' He sipped at his tea thoughtfully, seeming in much better humour this morning, although his tiredness was still showing.

Gina looked at him curiously, scanning his face as he watched Alex and Stella, trying to ascertain whether there was any suspicion or doubt reflected in his eyes. There was none, there was only his obvious love for his wife. Her stomach contracted uneasily because of her own suspicions.

'Not so old, Daddy,' she said lightly. 'At fifty-six, I should say you've got . . . well, at least thirty years of happily married life to look forward to.'

Harry barked out his laughter, carelessly ruffling her hair as he used to when she was a child. 'Thank you, Georgina! I'll hold you to that!'

'Er—Stella and Alex get on remarkably well, don't they?' She was probing. If Harry had any doubts at all, she would recognise them now. She watched him closely as he replied.

'Wonderfully! Isn't it nice?'

'Y-yes. Very nice.' She remembered something then, something she couldn't reconcile with her suspicions. 'I understand it was Alex who introduced you to Stella?'

'That's right. And I'll be eternally grateful to him for that.' He turned to her then, his eyes meeting directly with hers. 'Alex tells me that you and he got on like a house on fire. You like him, don't you?'

'Er—yes, he's quite nice.' She shifted uneasily as her father's gaze continued to penetrate.

'Humph! And you resent his good relationship with Stella!'

Harry's shrewdness shocked her but didn't surprise her. Her father was no fool. But Gina hadn't been thinking of her own resentment of the relationship. 'Do—don't you resent it, Daddy?'

'Good grief, no! Alex is my kind of man, strong, forthright. We *all* get on well. And Stella thinks the world of her brother-in-law . . .'

Brother-in-law? Gina had to bite her tongue to prevent herself from stupidly parroting the words. Alex Craig was Stella's brother-in-law? A dozen thoughts sped through Gina's mind. Why hadn't Alex told her this? Alex's brother was dead—when did he die? How long had he been married to Stella? When did he and Stella get divorced? How come Alex had maintained a friendship with his brother's ex-wife?

She looked at her father uncomprehendingly. What sort of strange situation was this? It seemed to break . . . well, generally accepted social rules, at least! But what of that? If Harry—if they were all happy with the situation, fine!

'You didn't know, did you?' Harry chuckled. 'That old devil Alex hadn't told you he's Stella's brother-in-law!'

Gina was furious with Alex. She felt inordinately stupid. Her father's acceptance of the situation, the fact that Alex and Stella were related—sort of—combined to quell her suspicions. She must have got the wrong end of the stick last night. This new information didn't clarify all that she had overheard—but at least she could discount any ideas of a romantic relationship between Alex and Stella. It would be difficult, but she really must try to stop distrusting Stella so much.

'If I were to hazard a guess,' her father was saying now, 'you said something very unpleasant about Stella, and Alex didn't tell you they were related so that it would make you embarrassed when you found out!' He roared with laughter.

Gina couldn't help smiling. One would have to go a long, long way to pull the wool over Harry Duncan's eyes. He was the best judge of character she had ever known. Alex Craig ran a close second, though . . .

She felt better now. Much better. If there were anything fishy going on, Harry would know about it. Impulsively she got to her feet and waved to the other two as they walked across the beach towards the bungalow.

'There's a good girl,' Harry said quietly. 'Make an effort, Georgina. Try and get along with Stella—if only for my sake.'

Stella was bubbling with enthusiasm as she approached. 'Harry, we've been to look at the house. It's almost finished! We'll be able to move in in a few weeks!'

'Wonderful!'

'That is good news, Stella.' Gina smiled at her stepmother and was immediately rewarded by Alex. He came to a halt by her side, bidding her good morning and slipping a casual arm around her waist, sending a delicious warmth coursing through her body.

'And Alex is flying me into Nairobi tomorrow,' Stella went on. 'I'm going to order furniture and things!'

'Splendid!' said Harry. 'I shan't be up to it, of course, but why not take Georgina with you? It'll make a nice change for her.'

Stella responded instantly. But there was just . . . was there just the slightest hesitation from Alex? 'Of course, you must come too, Gina.'

Gina stepped away from him. Was she getting paranoid, or was he slightly reluctant for her to join them? 'I won't, thank you.' Her tone was polite enough. 'There are one or two personal things I have to discuss with Daddy. Tomorrow will give me time to talk with him.'

CHAPTER SIX

'YOU'VE *what*?' Harry Duncan slammed down his coffee cup so hard that its contents spilled out into the saucer. They had just finished lunch, and Gina had finally made her announcement about dropping out of college. She'd put it off as long as she possibly could, expecting her father to be cross—but not expecting this sort of fury.

'What the devil are you talking about, Georgina? You can't just drop out of school when you've completed almost two years' training! Explain yourself!'

Gina squirmed uncomfortably. 'Daddy, I had one more term and one more year to go and . . . and I couldn't carry on. I couldn't stand another day of it. I don't belong there.'

'I've never heard such nonsense!' Harry bellowed. 'And as soon as these holidays are over, back you go—to school!'

'No, Daddy.' She was slightly afraid of him, but quietly determined. 'I've finished. I've told them—I've done it all officially. Please try to understand. Daddy, it was useless! I'm just not good enough to make it in . . .' Her voice trailed off as she saw the blood draining from her father's face. She reached out to him frantically, hating herself for upsetting him so much, for not waiting longer before she told him.

'Daddy?' The pallor of his face terrified her.

'Get me my pills!' His voice had grown hoarse. 'They're on the dressing table . . . the little brown bottle.'

Gina fled to his bedroom, drenched in remorse. Oh, why hadn't she waited until he was feeling better before she'd told him? Snatching hold of the pills, she dashed back to the patio, pouring some water with hands which were suddenly shaking.

Harry swallowed two tablets, his hand reaching to massage his heart as he breathed slowly, deeply.

'Daddy, please forgive me. I'm so sorry——'

'I'm all right,' he snapped. 'It's just that I'm not supposed to get so excited. Now then, explain yourself.'

'It—it doesn't matter,' she faltered. 'This can wait till some other time.'

'I'll be the judge of that. Start talking. What was this rubbish about not being good enough?'

Gina cringed inwardly. Harry had always wanted so much for her—expected so much of her—as far as education was concerned. After six months in art school, she'd known she would never make the grade. She had come to terms with it, but it would be very hard to make her father accept it.

'I wanted to become an illustrator,' she began patiently, 'but in that sphere and in all aspects of commercial art the competition is intense. Daddy, there are so many hundreds of people who are better than I. You just have to take my word for it. I've seen the work of my contemporaries, people from other schools, even first-year students. I'm not good enough to make it. It has to be faced.'

'What about painting? I don't mean illustrating and all that sort of stuff. Just straight painting? I've seen your work. I know you're good . . .'

'I'm a technician, Daddy,' she said softly, 'but that's all. I don't have the X ingredient which makes an artist successful. I wish I had, believe me. But even the best art school in London can't develop what isn't there in the first place. I'll never be more than a competent technician.'

Harry sighed unhappily. 'I see you've given this some thought. That's something, at least. I'd thought you were just being impetuous.'

'No, not at all. I know I'm doing the right thing. I had to leave. I didn't want to spend the next sixteen months being miserable. I love being surrounded by art—but I'll never earn a living producing it.'

'I'm not concerned about you earning a living.' Her father's voice was crisp now, authoritative. 'I want to know what you intend doing with the rest of your life, because I shall certainly not allow you to drift from one thing to the next. Do you hear me, Georgina? I want to see you settled.'

It was then that Gina told him of her plans for opening an art shop-cum-art gallery. But try as she would, she could not put any real enthusiasm into her voice. Somehow, at some point since her arrival in Africa the idea had lost its appeal. Not that she'd considered it the perfect solution for her in the first place. But it was something. It would be, at least, something to do with her life. And she needed that; she needed something to fill the loneliness, the emptiness of her life. An emptiness which she felt more acutely now she had started to love Alex Craig.

'And it wouldn't take a great deal of capital,' she said, with a gaiety which was forced. 'I could get things under way with about ten or fifteen thousand pounds. I'd need a good stock of artists' materials, of course, and I'd need money to convert the premises I'd rent. But I could get a lot of paintings on sale or return. And I've found the ideal place, by the way. I've even spoken to the landlord about it. It's in Kensington . . .'

She stopped abruptly. Harry was shaking his head in a resolute manner she was all too familiar with. The answer was no. There'd be no arguing with him now. No per-suading.

'But, Daddy, why? Why——'

'You're not cut out to be a business woman, Georgina. It wouldn't work—I'll tell you that for nothing. You'd be sick of it within two months.'

'That isn't fair! You can't possibly know that!' Gina surprised herself, actually, arguing for something she didn't really want in the first place. Her pride was hurt. She had hoped, at least, for a show of faith from her father.

His next words made her feel a little better. He had other reasons for refusing her. 'If you were expecting me to finance this venture—forget it. I have no spare capital, Georgina.'

She looked at him blankly. This was rather hard to believe, considering the price he'd got when he'd sold out his business last year!

'Don't look at me like that. I'm telling you straight. Have you ever known me lie to you? I don't like your ideas, but that's something quite separate from the fact that I can't let you have any money. For this or for anything else. I've sunk all my capital into a copper mine.'

The copper mine! Yes, she remembered Alex telling her about that. 'All your capital? Daddy, it isn't like you to put all your eggs in one basket.'

'True. But this is going to bring very big rewards when we hit pay dirt. When that happens, none of us will ever have to worry about money for the rest of our lives.'

Gina shrugged. Her father obviously knew what he was doing. It surprised her that he had invested such a great deal of money. She'd thought he would never have to worry about money for the rest of his life—with or without the mine. But that was Harry. Always the business man, always seeking to make more.

'. . . So you see,' he was saying now, 'apart from what I've kept aside to live on, and to get the new house in order, there's no spare cash. Georgina, are you still listening to me?'

She was and she wasn't. Frankly, at that moment she was thinking of herself, of the future which seemed barren and dull. What would she do with herself now?

Her father's next words didn't help one bit. 'You'd better put on your thinking cap, Georgina, and come up with a suggestion which will meet with my approval. I'm

not going to sit by and watch you turn into some sort of—
of hippie! Now then, if you'll excuse me, I'm going to lie
down for a while.'

Gina looked at him with eyes full of concern. Harry
was a disappointed man. He was disappointed in her, and
it made her feel guilty. She was sorry, too, that she hadn't
postponed this talk until a later day. He looked strained,
unhappy, and decidedly unwell. To add to her worries
was her knowledge that there had been an implicit threat
in his last words . . . if she didn't come up with some ideas
about what to do, he would. She remained on the patio
after he had gone, thinking, thinking, thinking. And getting nowhere.

It was almost seven o'clock when Alex and Stella
returned. Gina was lying on her bed, still trying to snatch
some of the sleep which had become so elusive to her. She
glanced at the clock when she heard Alex's car pull up, a
fleeting jealousy rushing through her because he had spent
more than twelve hours in Stella's company.

Without stopping to think of the futility of it, Gina went
to pains over her appearance that evening, putting on
one of the kangas she'd not yet worn and taking trouble
over her make-up. When Stella came into her room an
hour later, however, Gina felt like a little girl competing
in a grown-up game. Stella looked beautiful in a rose-
pink dress which flattered her undeniably perfect figure. Her
hair and make-up were soft and natural-looking, making her
appear ten years younger than she actually was.

'Good evening, Stella. Did you have a successful day's
shopping?' Gina smiled at her via the dressing table mirror.
For Alex, for her father's sake, she was making an effort to get
on with her stepmother. It didn't last long.

'I've ordered about half of the things I wanted, yes.
The bare essentials, at least. Of course, I'll have to go
into Nairobi again.' She gestured to a chair. 'May I sit
down, Gina?'

'Of course.' There was something on Stella's mind. That much was obvious, and while she was as gracious and polite as ever, Gina couldn't miss the spark of annoyance in her beautiful green eyes.

'Gina, I've been talking with your father. He's really upset. I'm here to ask you if you'll reconsider. Won't you go back to school and finish your training at least? To please him.'

Her audacity infuriated Gina. That, plus the fact that her father had been discussing her affairs with this—this stranger! 'This is none of your business, Stella! And I see my father's told you only half the story. There is no point whatever in my returning to school!'

Stella returned her gaze unflinchingly. 'It is my business! Anything that affects Harry is my business— please remember that. Especially where his health is concerned.'

Her firmness surprised Gina, and while she resented Stella's interference, she couldn't help acknowledging a certain respect for her protective attitude towards Harry. It was a respect Gina was not about to reveal, however. 'We have no more to discuss. Kindly leave me to finish dressing.'

'Very well.' Stella got to her feet, bowing her head in assent. 'I want us to be friends, Gina. I want that very much. And I'm not going to achieve it by hiding my feelings, so you might as well know that I think you were thoughtless and inconsiderate in breaking this news to your father today. You don't seem to appreciate how unwell he's been this past week, how upset he's been over Ralph. You could have waited at least another week before you gave him further worries.'

'Further worries?' Gina looked up in astonishment. 'My father doesn't worry over me! I'm perfectly capable of looking after myself.'

'I won't fight with you, Gina.' Stella's hand reached for the single strand of pearls around her neck in a nervous gesture. 'I'm aware that you've never seen much of your father, that you've never been really close to him. And I think that's a shame. But you can take my word for it, he worries about you very much.'

She left then, as graciously and quietly as when she had entered the room, her head held high but with a sad little smile hovering around her lips.

Gina glared after her, resentment outweighing her new-found respect. Maybe Stella did have a right to know what was going on, but she had no right to try and manipulate Gina. Harry was perfectly capable of that, without any assistance from Stella!

Gina hung back in her room, waiting until the last possible moment before joining the others in the lounge. Even so, she picked the wrong instant to emerge. Just as she stepped on to the verandah, Alex Craig was closing the door to his own bedroom.

He turned, his arm reaching out to stop her as she walked past him, bidding him good evening in her coolest voice. 'Why didn't you tell me you'd dropped out of school?' Deep blue eyes were scrutinising her face, as if he were at a loss to understand her.

'Oh, no, not you, too!' She tried to pull away from him but he held firmly to her wrist. 'Ye gods, does the whole of Malindi know I'm a drop-out?'

'What the hell is the matter with you?' The deep voice was rough with annoyance. 'I thought we were friends, but you've become so distant since your father got back. Why, Gina?'

'*I've* become distant?' she blurted. 'It's the other way round, Alex. You've hardly noticed I'm alive since your precious Stella got home!'

She regretted the remark instantly, not wishing to reveal in any way her feelings for him. Fortunately, Alex didn't interpret it as a comment from one who was jealous. He put it down to Gina's resentment of her stepmother.

'Don't be ridiculous! You might hate Stella's guts, but

that's your problem. She happens to be my sister-in-law, and I think very highly of her.'

'And how come you never told me you were related?'

'I tried to. Twice I was about to tell you on that first day, but you just went on ranting and raving about her, so I left it. Then it amused me to think of your embarrassment when you found out, after all your nasty remarks about her.'

'Well, I'm not. I don't retract anything I said.'

'Gina, don't let's fight.' His hands slid up her arms to her shoulders, holding them, caressing gently so that her legs became weak, her heart beating so loudly she was afraid he would hear it. 'I want to talk to you,' he said then. 'Let's go out for a drink after dinner. We can go into Malindi. There's something I want to discuss——'

'I don't see the point, Alex.' She smiled up at him then, trying to keep her voice light, casual. 'It's been really lovely knowing you. You're a nice man, contrary to what I thought in the beginning!' She laughed gaily, impishly, even as she cursed herself for falling in love with him. Maybe she had been the distant one of late. If so, it was just her way of protecting herself from a man who thought nothing of her, a man who could so easily break her heart.

She must, absolutely must, keep her distance now. She stepped back, moving away from the warmth and excitement of his hands. 'I'm going to telephone the airline in Nairobi tomorrow. It's time I was going home now.'

'But you'd planned on staying another week or so.' Still he seemed at a loss to understand her. Was he disappointed that she was leaving, or was he just being polite? He drew her towards him, his very nearness making her heady, affecting her senses. 'Gina, before you make that phone call, listen to what I have to say. Come out with me later and——'

They turned at the sound of approaching footsteps. It

was Harry. He stood at the end of the verandah, beckoning to them. 'Get a move on, you two,' he said gruffly. 'Dinner's been ready for fifteen minutes.'

Alex laughed, linking Gina's arm through his as he led her towards the lounge. Harry stood, watching them as they approached, an odd sort of look in his eyes which Gina couldn't interpret. Then he smiled at his daughter indulgently, broadly, as if to say that all was forgiven. Gina looked at him suspiciously, wondering what was going through his mind. He was up to something; she just knew it. Harry had spent the entire afternoon in his bedroom, no doubt mulling over his earlier conversation with Gina . . .

Only an hour ago, Stella had complained that her husband was very upset. He didn't look that way now; in fact he looked happier now than he had since his arrival from Australia. Gina's stomach contracted into a tight knot. Just what was Harry up to? It concerned her; it had to! Harry had organised and controlled her life from the moment she was born. What preposterous plans was he making for her now?

Preposterous turned out to be exactly the right word. Harry dropped his bombshell when they were halfway through the main course of their dinner. He had been quiet up till then, but he suddenly turned to Alex, smiling to himself as if he had just reached a satisfactory conclusion in his own mind, and addressed the younger man as if he were the only other person in the room.

'Alex, I've been thinking. Georgina is now at a loose end; I don't want her standing behind a shop counter for the rest of her life, nor do I wish her to run around with those wild people she's involved with in London. Now, you're looking for a wife. How about taking on Georgina?'

One could have heard a pin drop. The deafening silence stretched on and on for what seemed like an eternity. Gina gaped at her father as if he were an alien from another planet, while Stella lost all her composure and sat, staring, her fork suspended in mid air.

The two women exchanged looks and Gina saw her own blush reflected on her stepmother's face. The thought of marriage to Alex Craig was not a new one to Gina. She had indulged in several fantasies lately—of being married to Alex, of spending her days in his huge old house on top of the hill, of bearing his children and living peacefully, compatibly. That much, she was sure she could achieve with him. If only he could love her, if only . . .

The scene at the table was like a tableau, Gina's anger at her father rendering her speechless. Alex was watching her, a strange smile playing around his mouth. It was peculiar how the conversation went then. Had it not been for Stella's protest, her obvious disgust, Gina might have reacted very differently. As it was, she tried to counteract Stella's shock by putting it down as a joke.

'Harry!' Stella's fork almost dropped from her hand. 'That's the most appalling . . . How can you *do* this? You're even embarrassing me, so I can imagine how Gina feels!'

'I'm not embarrassed, Stella.' With difficulty Gina managed a smile. 'Just furious. But even that's beginning to fade, because I see now that my father is joking.'

'No,' Alex spoke calmly, 'he isn't, actually.'

Harry turned to the women, a look of impatience pulling his bushy eyebrows together. 'Keep out of this. I was addressing Alex. Well, young man, what do you think of the idea?'

Alex was not at all ruffled. He seemed to have trouble in taking his eyes from Gina, but when he finally turned to his friend, his look was one of resignation—mock resignation. 'I'm afraid someone's already beaten me to it. I can understand you wanting to see your daughter settled, but there's a man named Charles who——'

'Charles!' Harry scoffed before breaking into a loud guffaw. 'Charles St John? That wet upper-class twit! Is he still after you, Georgina?'

'Daddy! Charles is—I really think this has gone far enough!' Her face flushed with all the embarrassment she had earlier denied. In that instant she hated Alex Craig, hated him for mocking her like this. But she couldn't say anything! How could she attack him, without risk of revealing any of her feelings for him? That would really give him cause to mock!

As for her father ... if he were not a sick man, she'd really give him a piece of her mind! How dared he try to manipulate her like this? How could he embarrass her so? Did he really think he could continue to control her life like this, to the extent of involving another person in his—his latest idea of disposing of his daughter!

She was cornered, tongue-tied, frustrated to the point of tears. If only they knew how this was hurting!

Human nature being what it is, when Stella put in her opinion Gina lashed out at her viciously. It was then that all hell broke loose. Gina regretted her attack but was unable to prevent it. In thrashing out at Stella she was at least safe from revealing any of her deeper feelings.

'Stop it! Both of you!' It was the first time Stella had ever raised her voice. 'If this did start as a joke, it's certainly gone past it now! Harry, how can you talk about your daughter as if—as if she's not even present?'

'Thank you, Stella, but I don't need you to defend me. I can speak for myself.'

'Then why don't you?' Alex put in coolly. 'Let's hear your reaction to your father's idea. Personally—if anyone's interested—I think it quite a good one.'

Gina's head shot up in astonishment, her eyes scanning his in an effort to see whether he was still mocking. But Stella shot to her feet, ruining the moment completely. 'Are you crazy? Are you both mad? You're not talking about buying a wife for one of your servants. We're civilised people! In our society marriage must always include love! Without love, the marriage would be doomed!'

'I'm not too sure about that.' Gina's response came

smoothly, calculatingly. 'Love didn't seem to do you much good on the two previous occasions you've been married.'

Stunned, shocked into silence, Stella sank back into her chair as if she'd been slapped in the face. In that instant all Gina's resentment turned to hatred—of herself. Oh, how many times her acerbic tongue had got her into trouble! It was an unfair, unworthy remark. She had used Stella. She had used her as a means of saving her own pride. In her comment to Stella she had let Alex Craig know that love didn't enter her scheme of things, and she'd wanted to convey that to him because she thought— was almost sure—he'd been serious about thinking their marriage a good idea.

But when Alex turned to her then she was sure of nothing but his fury. His face was a tight mask of anger, a thin white line was etched around his lips, a muscle working in his jaw as if he were using every ounce of restraint not to get up from the table and beat her. She flinched as bright blue eyes raked her face. 'My God, Harry!' he hissed, not taking his eyes from her. 'If you hand your daughter over to me, I warn you now, I'll tame her! I'll teach her a few manners if it kills me! You've gone wrong with her—do you know that? Somewhere along the line, you've gone wrong, but by heaven, I'd take over where you left off!'.

Harry was watching him avidly, nodding, as if in agreement with every word Alex spoke. Until now he had seemed peculiarly detached, as if he had set into motion an intellectual game of ping-pong and had been quite content to sit back and watch things happen, let the sparks fly. 'You're right.' He slapped Alex on the shoulder. 'You're absolutely right! You're just the man for her. I knew it! She needs someone who can keep her in line. But she'll make a good wife——'

Gina got up so quickly that she knocked over her wine glass, her chair clattering to the floor as she bolted for the door. This was more than she could stand. Her father—

both men—were talking of her as if she were a chattel, a head of cattle!

She got no farther than the verandah when Alex caught up with her, his right hand reaching out to stop her in her tracks so roughly that her shoulder almost dislocated. He yanked her against him, his fingers biting into her flesh. 'Get back in there and apologise. Apologise to Stella! Now!'

'Go to hell!' She instantly regretted her movement as the pain of her twisted arm made her see stars.

Alex's mouth curled back in a snarl, the quietness of his voice a dangerous weapon in itself. 'If you were my wife ... if I took you on ...'

'Took me on?' she fumed. 'You make me sound like some sort of project! Don't worry, the last thing I need is a man like you!'

'Many a true word spoken in anger,' he countered. 'I would be the last thing you'd need. I'd make a woman out of you! You wouldn't need some silly little business to occupy your mind. You wouldn't be bored. You wouldn't drop out of life!' He pulled her towards him angrily, his eyes burning down into hers, his breath a warm fan against her face. 'I'd teach you what a woman should be. As the wife of Alex Craig, you'd learn who you are, know what was expected of you!'

His look turned to one of mockery, disgust. 'But you can't let go of Daddy, can you? You can't accept the fact that he's married Stella and has his own life to lead. You can't allow Stella to be your friend—when she wants it so much. The trouble is, Georgina, you just can't handle relationships. With anyone! As soon as we became friends, you shied off. To put it succinctly, dear girl, you are suffering from emotional constipation!'

And with that, he thrust her away from him, releasing his grip on her so abruptly that she staggered backwards. She stared after him dumbfounded, horrified at the cruelty of his words. Emotional constipation! What a horrible, wicked thing to accuse her of!

Once inside her bedroom, the tears started, her face crimson with humiliation at the shocking realisation that Alex might be right about her. She did have difficulty forming relationships. She always had!

She tore back the mosquito net, threw herself down on the bed and sobbed until there were no more tears left. She heard a car driving away, lights being switched off, the faint sound of voices from the next bedroom, and then silence. That still, eerie silence as the house, but not its inhabitants, settled down for the night.

When the soft knock came at her door, Gina didn't answer it. She turned over on to her stomach, burying her face against the pillow and willing her unwelcome caller to go away. Whoever it was.

There was a soft touch on her shoulder, the faint whiff of perfume as she turned to see Stella, her blue satin negligee swirling around her legs as she sat on the edge of the bed.

Gina's voice was barely more than a whisper. 'If you've come for an apology, you have it. I'm terribly sorry for my remark at dinner.'

'Please look at me.' Stella switched on the bedside lamp, her face troubled and as lovely as ever even without its make-up. 'I can't sleep, Gina. I—it's—I didn't come for an apology. What's more important to me is that you understand something. You see, I think you've got the wrong idea . . . I did love my previous husbands. I want you to know that.'

Gina kept her eyes averted, partly because she still didn't trust the woman and partly because she knew Stella was making an effort and she wasn't helping any. Was making it more difficult for her.

'Gina dear, when my first husband died, I never thought I'd love again, but life . . .'

'Died?' For the first time, Gina looked her straight in the eyes. 'You were still married to Alex's brother when he died?'

'Of course.' Delicate eyebrows drew together worriedly. 'Hasn't Alex told you about it? Hasn't he explained?'

'He told me nothing. I even had to find out from my father that you were related. I—I'd thought you were divorced from Alex's brother.'

Stella sighed resignedly. 'I'm afraid that's typical of Alex. He doesn't like to talk about the past—you must have noticed that about him.' Her eyes were pleading, hurt. 'I don't know what assumptions you've made about me. It—I suppose it's my fault. I should have told you more about myself when we first met. Harry knows everything, of course. But I want you to hear it from me. David—my first husband—died in a car crash after we'd been married for two years. I was in the passenger seat ... Gina, don't you know that I'm Kenyan, too? That I've come back here because this is my original country? I was brought up in——'

'No!' Gina's mouth fell open in surprise. 'I knew nothing of that. But your house in America—your accent!'

The older woman laughed softly, briefly. 'I moved to America after David's death. I had to. I couldn't bear Nairobi with all its ... its memories. I met my second husband when I was thirty—yes, it was years before I even looked at another man. I—I'd lost David when I was twenty-four. Alex was nineteen. Anyway, I married my second husband. Four years later, we were divorced. You see, I—I discovered I couldn't have children, and he—he was wealthy. He wanted an heir.'

She got up, padding softly around the room, recalling memories which hurt her. 'Oh, we told the law courts a different story, of course. But the real reason for our divorce was my inability to bear children ...'

Her voice trailed away. Gina looked down at her hands guiltily, glad that Stella had come into her room, appreciating the effort she had made in pointing out the truth. But she still couldn't feel close to her. Still she resented Stella's relationship with Alex, even though she understood it better now.

'I—thank you for coming, Stella. I know it wasn't easy for you. You must be shattered. I—I think we'd better say goodnight now.'

With a slight look of alarm Stella moved back to the bedside. 'There's something else I want to say. Please, please accept this in the right spirit, Gina. I—I want to say that I'll finance your business for you. I'd like to see you happy, and if that's what you——'

'Forget it. It's sweet of you, but my father would never allow it. Never. You should know him by now. Not only is he against the idea in principle, but he certainly wouldn't allow someone else to give me finance. He—he's very proud. He has some really old-fashioned ideas. He'd regard it as a blow to his pride—especially coming from his wife.'

Stella saw it immediately. 'You're right, of course. He is old-fashioned—though it's one of the things I love about him. He thinks he has to be the sole provider. But . . . I think he went too far tonight. Trying to marry you off! Alex would make a good husband, but I've told Harry not to mention it again—or rather, I asked him! Dear me, do you know what he said?'

Gina's eyes narrowed suspiciously. What was it about Stella that just didn't ring true? What was it that made Gina suspicious of everything? Her offer of finance, her insistence that Gina's marriage to Alex would be so wrong? She shook her head.

'He said it was strictly between him and Alex! That until you were twenty-one he would decide what was best for you. How Victorian can you get!'

'Very,' Gina said flatly. 'He's always been able to pressurise me into things.'

'Don't let him!' Stella's forcefulness took Gina by surprise. 'And I'll talk to Alex, too. Talk some sense into him! Don't worry, Gina, I'll fix it——'

'Leave it!' Gina's voice was brusque. Stella was advocating that a loveless marriage would be doomed. What she didn't know, of course, was that the marriage would not be loveless. At least . . . not wholly. But it wasn't that which made Gina so curt. What she resented was the idea of someone else trying to interfere. 'Leave it, Stella. If anyone talks to Alex, it will be *me*.'

She didn't expect that to happen quite so quickly, though. At four o'clock in the morning Gina found herself in that familiar spot outside, wide awake and alert, with only the moon for company . . . until Alex appeared from the doorway of the lounge.

Gina started, her heart pounding from shock even though he moved silently. In one hand he held a glass of brandy, in the other hand a beer. 'Peace offering.'

She looked at him stupidly as he handed her the beer, lowering himself on to the seat beside her. 'Where—what are you doing here at this time of night?'

He was smiling, and yet again she was surprised at his ability to shed his temper. Why wasn't he still cross with her . . . why didn't she feel cross with him?

'I was in the lounge. Waiting up for you.' He laughed at the look on her face. 'I've watched you, Gina. Night after night you come out here, pacing around like a lost spirit.'

'What—what do you want, Alex?'

'I want to talk about that scene at dinner tonight.'

'Oh! Well, I'm sorry if you were embarrassed. Let me apologise right now, on my father's behalf. You see, he doesn't know what to do with me now I've left school.' Her voice was bitter, angry. 'There are no more schools he can put me into, so he came up with this idea of marriage—the ultimate institution!'

'Take it easy,' Alex ordered. 'Just calm down and listen. Now, I mentioned earlier that I wanted to talk to you,

remember? Well, as a matter of fact, I was going to talk
to you about marriage. You see, I'd had the idea before
Harry. He preempted me at dinner time. And I don't
care for another man making a proposal for me, even if it
is someone as special as Harry.'

Gina's heart constricted so that it seemed to stop, the
blood pounding in her ears so she had to strain to hear
him.

'I want you to forget that scene at the dinner table,
Gina. I want you to disregard your father's pressures. This
proposal is coming from *me*, not him. So please consider it
with an open mind.'

She didn't dare to speak and even as her mind was
screaming in assent, disappointment brought her heart to
life again. He was being so—so businesslike!

'You once told me you'd consider marriage if you had
nothing better to do. Remember?'

When she didn't reply, he repeated his statement.
'Remember?'

'I—Y-yes. Yes, that's right.'

'Well, you have nothing better to do. You've refused to
return to college and Harry's blocked your business ideas.
I've been looking for a suitable wife since I was thirty.
You're suitable—no, don't look at me like that, it's true.
Consider: we have, basically, a great deal in common.
Think about it. Think about how well we get on.'

She didn't need to think about it. They did get on—
when they were away from the influence of other people.
The idea of spending her life with Alex Craig was more
than she had dared hope for. During her time in Africa,
in his company, on this . . . this voyage of self-discovery
she had come a long, long way. She had found that which
had been missing, that which had filled her with a name-
less longing. She didn't need any more education, she
didn't need a business. She needed Alex Craig.

'You've made it very plain to me about your ideas of
what a marriage should be. I've noted all of it. I would

expect you to run my house, act as hostess to my guests, be my companion. You would be a wife to me in every respect.' He broke off and smiled that lazy, insolent smile of his. 'But I'm sure we'd have no problems in that department. I wouldn't keep you prisoner. You'd have the freedom you wanted, and we could travel together. I think I can promise you wouldn't be bored.'

With every sentence he spoke, Gina's heart sank deeper and deeper. Love didn't enter into it. Love—or anything remotely approaching it. He wanted her for his wife. Why? Because he'd been looking for the past three years. Because he was lonely.

'I'm not starry-eyed about this, about anything in fact. Any more than you are, Gina. You're a practical girl, level-headed. So think about it, will you?'

'I-I'll think about it,' she managed, hating him, loving him, knowing then what her answer would be, and praying that her love would be enough for both of them. 'I'll give you an answer tomorrow.'

Then, bludgeoning her well-hidden emotions with a final word, a word which should have served as a warning to her, 'And bear in mind that if you hate being married— well, it isn't irreversible.'

'That's true,' she said levelly. 'And bearing that in mind, why didn't you suggest we just live together?'

Alex looked mildly surprised. She wanted desperately to hear him say that that would not be good enough. That he *wanted* to make a commitment, albeit only a legal one. That he was prepared, at least, to think in terms of permanence.

But he didn't. 'We couldn't do that,' he said calmly, with a dismissive wave of his arm. 'Your father would have a blue fit.'

CHAPTER SEVEN

THEY were married three days later, for the price of a few Kenyan shillings, during a simple little ceremony that took all of fifteen minutes to complete. Gina wore the white lacy dress she had bought in Nairobi, Alex an off-white safari suit, while Stella and Harry were dressed formally in attire which would have been more fitting for a wedding in one of the world's finest cathedrals.

Fifteen minutes, and now she was no longer Gina Duncan but Mrs Alexander Craig. Fifteen minutes—that was all it took to change not only her name but her entire future. As Alex slipped the broad band of gold on to her wedding finger, Gina's hand trembled with a mixture of joy and trepidation.

She glanced over at the two people who had witnessed the wedding. Her father, nodding, confident, beaming broadly as if this were the best thing he'd seen since his own wedding. Stella, unsmiling, motionless, her anxious eyes protesting that she thought this a mistake, a mistake! Who was right? Which one of them? Only time would tell.

They stepped out into the blazing April sunshine, congratulations pouring heartily from the lips of Gina's father; automatically, stiffly, from the lips of her stepmother. A solitary photographer leaned lazily against the wall of the building, springing to life as the bride and groom appeared, his camera clicking busily. Harry shooed him away, muttering under his breath about the tenacity, audacity of the press.

Gina turned, her hand reaching out for that of her husband. But he was otherwise engaged. Resentment flooded over her as she saw Stella stepping into his open arms, watched the claiming and giving of the traditional, mandatory kiss. For a moment, time seemed to slip backwards. In Gina's head there were echoes of a conversation she had overheard; in her heart there was the stirring of suspicions she thought she had quelled. What *was* it with those two? Why was Alex so enamoured of the wife of his best friend?

Then her husband was by her side, linking her arm through his as he led the way to the car. For an awful moment she wanted to pull away from him, to thrash out at him for his casualness, to scream in protest at the unfairness of being head over heels in love with a husband who did not love her.

Alex smiled down at her then, as if sensing something was amiss. His arm slipped around her waist in a familiar gesture. The gesture was familiar, but Gina's reaction was not. At the feeling of his arm encircling her, a cold fear crept inside her. She knew it was irrational. She knew it would not last. But it prompted her to think of the night that lay ahead, and her reaction to that thought was one of anxiety, an inexplicable nervousness.

Perhaps not so inexplicable. It would be, after all, the first time for her. Surely she was entitled to have wedding-night nerves? Surely it was normal. Everything would be all right. From experience she knew that once she was locked in the embrace of her husband all other thoughts would melt away and she would give of herself happily, willingly—even wantonly.

'Well, I hope they remembered to put the champagne on ice!' Harry's voice broke into Gina's thoughts. 'Apart from wanting to toast the happy couple, I'm gasping for a drink!'

They were heading for the Sindbad Hotel. There they would have a wedding luncheon before flying off to Nairobi. To add to the peculiarity of this day was the fact that Harry and Stella would be travelling with them. They were going to collect a car Harry had been waiting for. A phone call from the dealers the previous day had sealed this arrangement. Harry and Stella would collect the imported car and drive the three hundred and sixty miles back to Malindi with an overnight stop somewhere en route. Stella had protested at the wrongness of this arrangement, saying they could use the commercial airline and fly up any other day. But Alex had insisted. It was silly, he had said, to use the commercial line when he could so easily give them a lift.

Throughout lunch the champagne flowed, and Gina drank more than her fair share of it in an effort to take the edge of the nervousness crawling around her insides. It didn't help. It served only to give her a mild headache which would make the flight to Nairobi less enjoyable. What the alcohol didn't do for Gina, however, it did for Stella. Already she seemed to have got used to the fact that the marriage had taken place. She chatted easily, even gaily, throughout the meal, more than making up for Gina's quietness.

'. . . And we're going to have a big housewarming party when we move in, aren't we, Harry?'

'If that's what you want, dear, yes. I suppose you've started planning for it already? It'll only be a matter of weeks before we vacate Alex's house.'

'I have. We'll ask all our neighbours along the beach, a couple of my old friends from Nairobi and . . .' she turned to Alex then, 'Mr and Mrs Craig! You will come down, won't you?'

'Of course, darling.' Alex leaned over and patted her hand affectionately. Gina looked on, telling herself that if they could behave like this in her presence, and that of her father, there couldn't possibly be anything wrong going on between them.

By the time they landed at the Nairobi aerodrome, Gina's heart was like a stone. It isn't irreversible—that was what Alex had said, the night of his proposal. It isn't irreversible

. . . Dear Lord, she didn't want to reverse anything! She loved Alex Craig. She wanted desperately to make of their marriage the success she knew it could be.

Why, then, was the idea of sleeping with him tonight filling her with dread?

The sight of the house coming into view made her spirits lift enormously. It was like coming home. Kimau stood in the open doorway, tall, erect, smiling broadly as he beckoned forward a young houseboy to take the newly-weds' luggage.

'Memsab!' Kimau bowed from the waist, taking Gina's hand only when she offered it. 'Welcome home.'

'Thank you, Kimau. Thank you very much.' She was touched by the obvious pleasure in the old man's eyes.

'Bring your wife to the house some time,' Alex said unexpectedly. 'We will have a celebratory drink.'

Delighted, Kimau bowed again and backed away from them.

'He has a wife?' Gina turned to her husband in surprise. 'But I thought he lives in?'

Alex grinned. 'He has one wife, yes. She lives on Kimau's *shamba*, a few miles from here. He has his own piece of land, you see. His wife lives there with their children and their grandchildren. The family look after the land—until such time as Kimau retires from working here, and joins them permanently.' He shrugged. 'Kimau has worked for the Craigs since before I was born. He's as much a part of this house as I am. I can't see him ever retiring. Hmm, don't look so puzzled, Gina. Kimau sees his wife when I give him time off. Soon, I'll explain to you the ways of the Kikuyu people, and you'll understand things better.'

'I look forward to that,' she smiled. 'In the meantime, all I want is a cup of tea.'

Alex threw back his head and laughed. 'All that coffee growing outside, and my wife wants a cup of tea!'

My wife. How strange, even alien those words sounded.

They had tea on the verandah at the back of the house, outside the lounge. The conversation was one-sided. Gina was grateful to Alex for his constant chatter about the household and the running of it, although she didn't really register all he said, she was too preoccupied. She marvelled at her husband's relaxedness, his casualness; it was almost as if he brought home a new wife every day of the week.

'Hello, look who's here!'

Gina turned in her seat. Dashing up towards them was a long-legged, short-haired mongrel with a craggy face and sad-looking eyes. 'Whose dog is this?' she asked, reaching down to pat him.

'Mine—the servants'—the workers'—nobody's! He lives here and there, on my land. Gets fed wherever he can. He's a vagabond. I'm honoured if he comes to the house once a week.'

'What's his name?'

'Jacob.' He grinned. 'He's a sooner.'

'A sooner?'

'Mm. He'd sooner be out than in.'

Her laughter was a momentary release from tension. But she laughed too loudly, too long. She looked up to find Alex watching her carefully, the shadows of the house casting mysterious lights across his handsome features, his eyes seeming deeper, bluer than ever. 'Are you all right, Gina?' The deep voice was puzzled rather than concerned.

'Yes. A little tired. In fact I—I'd like to have a sleep before dinner. If you don't mind . . .'

'Not at all. It's been a long day. I'll show you to our room.'

Our room. She trailed behind him up the wide, curving staircase which led from the huge hallway of the house. What would it be like, actually sharing a bed with a man? Our room. He stopped in the doorway, pointing out the en-suite bathroom, the bell-rope hanging from a corner, should she wish to summon one of the servants.

'I have one or two things to do,' he said then. 'I'll come up around eight to get changed for dinner, okay?'

She nodded, unable to think of anything to say.

There were two huge bowls of flowers in the room. Kimau using his initiative? Or put there on Alex's instructions? There were no mosquito nets. They weren't necessary in Nairobi. Nor would it be so hot during the evenings.

This part of the house was already cool, already in shade. Gina walked over to the doors which opened on to the verandah. Here, from the first floor of the house, she could see even more of the magnificent scenery which would never fail to thrill her every time she looked at it. She couldn't wait to paint it: the craggy outline of the Ngong Hills, the richness of the land with its rows and rows of coffee bushes. There was a wealth of colour, of light and shade and form.

She stepped back into the room, closing the doors and half closing the curtains. On the bed there lay the unopened, beautifully wrapped package which Stella had thrust into her hands when they had parted. Everything else had been unpacked and put away for her. She opened one of the doors of the wardrobes which ran the full length of a wall. Alex's clothes. Inside the next section: her clothes. It was their room. On the dressing table there were Alex's hairbrushes, and her hairbrushes. In the vast bathroom there were two showers, one bath, one bidet and twin basins. Above them, on little glass shelves, were Alex's things, Alex's toothbrush. Her toothbrush.

The implications, the very intimacy of it made her stomach contract nervously. For her, this was a whole new world. A new country, a new status, an entirely different way of life. It excited her and scared her at the same time. She loved Alex Craig but he was, after all, virtually a stranger to her.

Plucking halfheartedly at the wrapping paper on Stella's gift, she sighed deeply. She wouldn't sleep. Not now. Not today, of all days. She'd just needed this time alone to try and rationalise her fears.

It was a pure white silk nightdress and negligee set. It was typical Stella. In fact it must have been something Stella had intended for herself; she couldn't possibly have found such a set in Malindi. So it was nice of her to give it to Gina. Nice of her to think of giving a gift when there had been so little time for such preparations.

Gina laid the set out on the bed, looking down at it dubiously. How would she look in it? What would Alex . . .

There would be no holding back tonight. This marriage had been sanctioned, not only by law but by Harry Duncan! Alex would claim her tonight not only because he wanted to, but because it was his right. It would be expected of her.

Something inside Gina was growing colder by the minute. Why, *why* was everything so different now? How could she want Alex so much with her body, while she recoiled from him in her mind? It didn't make sense, especially when she remembered what had happened in the room beneath this one barely a week ago!

But it had all been so different then. She had not been his wife. Alex had expected nothing of her. Then, she wasn't even aware of the depth of her feelings for him. Yet she had been carried away—wanting to give herself freely, even though she would have regretted it the following day.

She lay back on the bed, a cold sweat breaking out on her forehead. Tomorrow there would be nothing to regret. Tonight would be a consummation of their marriage. Their *marriage*. So why was she feeling like this, afraid, reluctant . . .? It was too ridiculous. Too—perverse!

'I enjoyed it very much.' Gina pushed back her plate,

picking up the wineglass which had been filled by her husband three times. She could feel the effects of the rich ruby liquid. It was slowing her down, making her body relaxed. But her mind was as sharp as a razor.

'But I'll bet you can make some improvements.' Alex smiled at her over the rim of his glass.

She could. And she would. She didn't want to enter this household like a new broom, didn't want to alter the way things were run. There were two servants who kept the place clean and did the washing and ironing. The cook worked part-time, and was Indian. And yes, she would teach him a thing or two, tell him to lighten his hand as far as his use of spices was concerned! But she would do that in her own time, in her own way. She wanted everything to carry on as normal. Any alterations she made would be subtle, gradual. Kimau had worked there for ever, had overseen the running of the house since before Alex was born. So Gina was not about to make him feel like a redundant old man.

'And your day is spent working the land, I suppose?' It seemed ludicrous, in the circumstances, that she had to ask such a basic, everyday question. But this was hardly an everyday sort of marriage.

'Yes, and I spend a couple of hours each day in the study, doing the books, making phone calls. Occasionally I go into Nairobi. Sometimes we get customers visiting the plantation—more as an excuse for a holiday on expenses than for any other reason. But that's okay. We'll entertain them here, put them up if necessary. As for the social life—well, that will be whatever you make of it. I know hundreds of people, as you can imagine . . .'

He lifted the bottle of wine; the second bottle. Gina shook her head. She'd already drunk too much. '. . . And there's always a barbecue, a party, something happening somewhere. Personally, I don't go in for much socialising, but . . .' he bowed his head and grinned at her, '. . . I'll leave that up to you. Bearing in mind our agreement, I'm prepared to go out more if you wish.'

It seemed to Gina a curious sort of conversation. Here they were, on their wedding night, trying to compromise as to what marriage should be, getting to know one another . . .

'I shan't demand much of you in that respect.' She smiled impishly. 'I like my quiet evenings at home. I bet that surprises you, mm? From one or two things my father said, you must have thought I lived the life of Riley in London!'

Alex didn't comment on that. 'About London—is it going to be very complicated to sort things out there? I mean, your flatmates have to be told that you're not going back. And let's not forget—Charles.'

There was something in his inflection that irritated her. 'I haven't forgotten Charles. I shall write to him very soon. And there's no problem as far as the flat's concerned. It's owned by one of my friends. She'll simply advertise for someone else. Not that she needs the money from a third person. She and Dinah might carry on as they are, just the two of them. Anyhow, I'll ask Sue to post a few things to me. The rest of my stuff can be thrown away for all I care. There's nothing—nothing I need that's still in London.'

She paused as the truth of her words struck home. There was nothing for her in London. There never had been. Everything she needed in life was right here, sitting across the table from her now.

'Shall we take coffee in the lounge?' he asked then, 'or would you rather have it here? Perhaps you'd like a stroll?' He laughed at what he was about to say next. 'After we've had coffee, we can take a stroll through the coffee.'

They settled in the lounge, the conversation slipping on to general matters. For all the world they appeared like a couple who had been married two, five, ten years . . .

It seemed that every time Gina glanced at her watch,

another half-hour had sped by. And with every passing minute she grew tenser and tenser. Knowing that men's attitude towards sex was fundamentally different from women's didn't help much. It was something they could just—just do. Coldly, unemotionally even, driven by a basic, animal need which excluded the necessity of love, feelings.

How different it was for women. For Gina, at least. She wanted to be made love to—not just sex. She wanted this to be a perfect, proper wedding night. She wanted to be told she was beautiful, desirable, *loved*. But it wouldn't be. It couldn't be. And she'd walked into this situation with her eyes wide open . . .

It was then that she finally understood herself. She couldn't give herself to Alex, because he didn't love her. Had he given her as much as a sign of his affections, then maybe. Probably. But he had not. And when she came to think about it, he hadn't even *told* her he was fond of her, hadn't even used an endearment. Not once. Yet they slipped from his lips so readily for his sister-in-law . . .

'. . . I'll lock up and join you in about fifteen minutes.' She looked at him stupidly as his words penetrated. This was it. He'd just suggested they turned in for the night. She must try to relax. She must! She must try to get close to her husband in every sense of the word. If she couldn't do that much, surely their marriage would be doomed. Doomed . . . Damn you, Stella, for your foresight!

Stupidly, irrationally, she damned her stepmother again as she picked up the nightdress and negligee, shoving them to the back of the wardrobe as if they were contaminated. She put on a cotton nightie which had been made with anything but seduction in mind. In the bathroom she quickly removed her make-up, brushed her teeth as if there were a time limit on doing the task.

She was in bed, trembling, the covers pulled up to her neck, by the time she heard Alex's footsteps on the stairs. Hysteria rose within her. She wanted to laugh and cry at the same time. What a ridiculous, ludicrous situation this was!

When she heard the distant ringing of the telephone, the first thing she did was to look at her watch. It was midnight. Who on earth could be ringing at this hour—on Alex's wedding night? Reprieve. The footsteps on the stairs halted, then faded away as Alex went to answer the telephone.

Gina got out of bed and flung open the French windows, feeling lightheaded and hot despite the chill night air. She stepped out on to the verandah, holding on to the rail—and Alex's voice came floating up to her as clearly as if he were standing beside her. It startled her. Alex must have made an excuse about locking up, in order to give her time to undress in private, because he had obviously left the lounge windows wide open. She could hear every word he said.

'No, I wasn't in bed. No, you couldn't have picked a better moment, actually. I was just on my way up-stairs . . .' Whoever was ringing had at least had the good grace to apologise. Gina stood at the edge of the verandah, breathing in the sweet, balmy night air. She hadn't intended to eavesdrop, it just happened. But Alex's next words brought her head up sharply.

'Where are you? It's a bit risky, phoning like this . . . I suppose Harry's asleep? . . . You're in reception? Then you'd better make this brief, you might be overheard.'

Harry? Did he say Harry was asleep? Heavens, it was Stella! What the devil . . .?

'And how did you manage that, when Harry was with you? . . . I see. I see. Yes. So you've transferred the money into my account—good girl. Thank you!'

Stella had transferred money into Alex's account? What money? How much money? And what for? Gina was trembling from head to toe. Just what was going on be-tween those two? She was suddenly chilled to the bone, but she couldn't, wouldn't move. There was no mistake this time, no room for ambiguity. What she had just heard was crystal clear.

Was Alex using Stella in some way? Was that why he was so attentive towards her? No, no, his fondness was not false, of that Gina was sure.

There was more to come:

'. . . Stella, it's a bit late to suggest that. Okay, maybe it is a mistake . . .'

Gina gasped, horrified. Damn Stella! How dared she ring up at this hour on someone's wedding night? How dared she tell Alex it was all a mistake!

She stepped back indoors smartly as she heard him bid Stella a fond farewell. Quickly closing the doors, drawing the curtains, she got back into bed, her heart pounding against her ribs.

Deceit! That's what she was up against. Something was happening that both she and her father should know about. Maybe it was innocent . . . No, if it were innocent, why keep it a secret? If Alex needed money, why not tell Harry? Harry would help. No . . . she remembered then that her father had no spare capital. Perhaps this wasn't a loan. Perhaps Stella was giving Alex money . . .

Gina drew a deep breath, bracing herself. She was not prepared to start out like this. If Alex were in some sort of financial crisis, she wanted to know about it. She was his wife, and she did not wish to start married life with secrets, deceit.

She was going to tackle Alex about this, just as soon as he walked through the door.

But when Alex came into sight, her nerve weakened. He was smiling, smiling broadly as if everything were just fine. 'Did you hear the phone ring? Sorry about that.'

For just a moment, her heart leapt to life. He was going to tell her! Thank God! He was going to volunteer——

'It was an overseas call—business. These foreigners tend to forget what time it is when they're calling overseas . . .'

He walked towards the bed, his hands reaching out for hers.

'Over—over . . .' She couldn't complete the word. He was lying to her! Lying in his teeth! All the love she felt for him was suddenly eclipsed by something approaching hatred. He was lying! All her fears, her confusion, her doubts and anxieties came back with a vengeance. They had never really left her. Adding to that the fact that Alex was lying to her, it wasn't surprising that she froze. Mentally and physically she recoiled, averting her head and pulling her hands from his clasp.

'Gina—what's wrong? Your hands are like ice!' He reached for her, but she stiffened, her back rigid against the pillow. His eyes, his voice were full of concern. But it was too late. Too late! 'Gina, what is it? What's wrong?'

'I—I'm tired, Alex. I——' It was all she could do to speak to him.

'Tired?' He laughed softly. 'Dear girl, this is our wedding night!' Dear girl? What a stupid, patronising expression that was! What did it mean? Nothing!

His arms slipped around her, pulling her closer, strong and warm and purposeful. But there was no comfort in his embrace. There was—nothing. He let go of her gently, blond eyebrows pulling together in a frown, deep blue eyes searching her face so she could hardly bear to look at him. She turned her head away, slumping back against the pillows like one who was desperately ill.

'Gina . . .?' He seemed alarmed. Then he laughed quietly, smiling as if he understood something she did not. 'Hey, take it easy, will you?' His finger traced the outline of her jaw, pausing under her chin to tilt her face towards his. 'What is this? Wedding night nerves? Dear girl, if it's any consolation to you, I understand. I know how it is. You don't really think I took in all that propaganda about your being a woman of the world, do you? Gina, you're nineteen years old, I don't expect you . . .'

His voice trailed away. His warm hands covered her

ice cold ones. She wanted to hit out at him, but she couldn't move. She wanted to scream at him, accuse him, but she couldn't speak.

'I'll get undressed,' he said dully. 'And for heaven's sake stop worrying. It'll be all right. We'll just lie together. I'll just hold you——'

'Alex!' Panic brought forth her voice. 'I—I don't want to sleep with you. I mean, I don't want to be in the same bed. I—I'll go to the guest room . . .' She swung her legs from the bed as he moved away. But his hand was on her shoulder, preventing her from getting up.

'My God, you mean it!' He lowered himself on to the bed, sitting beside her, finally registering the stiffness of her body, the dullness in her eyes. 'So you regret it already, eh? Gina, you're not giving it much of a chance, are you? For heaven's sake, I didn't anticipate this! I thought—this—would be the least of our problems. Can't you——'

'I'm not regretting the marriage, if that's what you mean.' It was true. Despite everything, she couldn't honestly say she regretted marrying him. It was just that there was so much she didn't understand, about herself, about him . . . 'I—I just need time, Alex. Let me, give me——' She didn't know what she wanted to say. Give me time? Give me an explanation? Tell me what's going on between you and Stella? Tell me how you *really* feel about her? Tell me you love me?

He got to his feet, letting out a long, slow breath. 'I understand.' His voice was resigned, but not annoyed. 'Believe it or not, I do understand how you feel, what you mean. You sleep here, I'll take the guest room.'

'No, I'll——'

'Do as you're told. It's all right. Don't worry about this. Try and get a good night's sleep.' His laugh was hollow, his smile sad. 'I'd planned on curing your insomnia tonight, but—well, I suppose you can live with it for one more day.'

CHAPTER EIGHT

ALEX's remark was still ringing in her ears at noon the following day. What a typically chauvinistic remark! Did he think that sex would be the cure-all? Did he think it would suddenly turn this marriage into what it should be?

Gina was sitting by the swimming pool. The table at her side was set for lunch, but Alex had not returned from Nairobi. She had been told by Kimau that Bwana would be back for lunch. She sat patiently. Waiting. Longing to see him and dreading it at the same time. There was another implication in his remark, of course. The implication that Alex had gone along with her for a mere twenty-four hours—which meant that she would have the same trauma to face all over again tonight.

She picked up her pineapple juice, sipping it thoughtfully. She was on very dangerous ground. Alex had made it clear that he expected her to be his wife in every sense of the word. And she wanted to be. How on earth could she get closer to him emotionally if she couldn't get close to him physically?

'Good morning!' The sound of his voice made her bristle. She turned, shading her eyes against the glare of the sun as she watched him approach. A dozen emotions churned inside her, all at variance with one another. Resentment, love, an overwhelming gratitude that he was safely home—and the fear that she would have nothing to say to him.

He looked superb, the epitome of health and fitness. He settled beside her, his eyes, his lips smiling. He wore a navy blue shirt which was open at the top, revealing the mat of blond hair on his chest. His slacks were tight, white, pulling against the masculine tautness of his thighs as he sat. Her eyes travelled over his hair, the little curls at the base of his neck, the strong column of his throat, the width of his shoulders and his tanned arms with their shirtsleeves rolled back. And his hands, hands that could excite her to the point of . . .

'Sorry I've been so long. What did you do with yourself this morning?'

She followed his lead, keeping her voice as light and casual as his own. 'I went walking through the *shamba*. Well, part of it, at least! It'd take a day or more to cover all of it.'

'Sure would. Did you get acquainted with anyone?'

'Only Jacob. He was sitting on the steps when I came out. We must be very honoured, having visits on two consecutive days!'

'He must have taken a fancy to you. Where is he now?'

'Ah, he's fickle.' She giggled as her nervousness started to disappear. 'He's left me for someone else. Vanished. Just like that!'

Kimau came to them then, carrying a tall glass of Scotch and soda with stacks of ice. 'Can I get anything for you, *memsab*?'

'No, thank you.' She smiled up at him, noticing the grace with which he moved, despite his extraordinary height and thinness.

'At what time would you like lunch?' He was addressing Alex, but Alex nodded towards Gina.

'Oh! Er—in half an hour.'

He bowed his head, smiling that famous Kenyan smile.

'I'll have to learn Swahili, I suppose. The other housemen don't speak English, do they?'

'Very little.' Alex laughed. 'Swahili will do, but if you really want to communicate with them, you'd better learn Kikuyu!'

'Oh, heavens! I'll take it one at a time, then.'

Neither of them noticed the visitor approaching. She obviously hadn't waited to be announced—had just walked around the house and sailed over to the swimming pool with the familiarity one might expect of one's nearest neighbour.

'Good morning!' Mandy Miller came to a halt, draping herself on to a chair without waiting to be invited. She was waving a newspaper which she immediately unrolled and placed on the table between Alex and Gina. It was clear to Gina, at least, that Mandy was doing her level best to hide her anger. 'Well, I must say this came as a surprise!' She gestured dramatically towards the photograph on the front page of the Nairobi morning paper. It was a good photograph, and underneath it there was a short article about the marriage of Nairobi's most eligible bachelor to Miss Georgina Duncan, daughter of the wealthy Englishman who had recently settled in Malindi.

'I thought I'd better give you the morning to yourselves,' Mandy said, with a smile which was obviously false, 'but I couldn't wait to come over and congratulate you.' She was wearing a pink halter-neck top and matching shorts, gold sandals and the full complement of gold jewellery she had worn on the beach that night.

'Thank you.' Alex smiled graciously. 'Can I pour you some juice, or would you like something stronger?'

'I'll have a gin and tonic, darling. Can't toast the happy couple with pineapple juice, can I? Well, Miss—Gina, what have you to say for yourself?'

'What do you mean?' The question came from Alex, his eyes flitting over to his wife, who had said nothing so far.

'Oh, I think Gina knows what I mean.' Mandy went into her posing routine, crossing and uncrossing her long legs and draping her arms across the back of her chair. 'She'd given me the impression that she wasn't interested in marriage.'

Alex frowned. He hadn't been present during that particular exchange on the beach. 'Really? Well, that's women for you!'

It was sweet of Alex. Gina appreciated how he had handled that one, and she followed his lead, smiling sweetly at the scantily-clad sex kitten as she waved a dismissive hand. 'It's a woman's privilege to change her mind. You must know that as well as I, Mandy.'

'But of course!' Mandy threw back her curly blonde hair, the smile on her lips belied by the icy glint in her eyes. 'I was only joking, my dear. Anyone can see you and Alex have fallen head over heels in love!'

In that instant, Gina knew a sensation of pure hatred. What a bitch! She'd come over here on a fishing expedition; she knew full well that Alex Craig was not in love with his wife.

But Alex continued to treat his neighbour as he had done before, courteously, attentively.

'Well, I hope this won't stop you from attending our monthly shoot, Alex. It's always been such fun! It'll be even nicer now, with the three of us.' Mandy spoke with a gaiety which was forced. Couldn't Alex see that? Probably not. Mandy Miller oozed sex appeal. It would be difficult for any man to see past that pretty face, the curvaceous body which she exploited to its best advantage.

Yet, perversely, Gina was almost glad of Mandy's presence. She provided a distraction—albeit a dangerous one. After all, how long could Gina keep up a private conversation with Alex without broaching on to deeper subjects?

That turned out to be easier than expected, however. During lunch, by which time Mandy had left, and for an hour afterwards Alex chatted on about his work force, his foreman, the plantation and how it functioned. True, he was encouraged by Gina's questions; but she wasn't asking idly, she was genuinely interested.

That evening, dinner passed pleasantly, too. Until Alex brought up the subject of a honeymoon . . .

Gina had slept for two solid hours during the afternoon, while Alex was in his study. She woke up feeling refreshed, alive—until the memories set in and an inner panic took control of her. It was curious, the way she felt as she dressed for dinner. It was as if her emotions had been put into deep freeze. Nothing was different. Her love for Alex, her resentment of him, her fears—it was all there, just as it had been the previous night. Nothing had changed. Nothing had advanced, nothing had regressed.

They were in the lounge, and Alex was pouring out their after-dinner brandies when he mentioned the idea of a honeymoon. Gina was on the settee, reasonably relaxed—until Alex came to sit beside her. 'I think we should go away,' he said, taking her by surprise. 'Have a holiday—a honeymoon.'

He looked at her expectantly, but Gina lowered her eyes, her hands fiddling nervously with the brandy glass. 'You see, when I'm here, I feel obliged to work. And there are phone calls, interruptions, people demanding things of me. It isn't giving us much of a start. I'd like to be alone with you, Gina. If we took the traditional honeymoon, if we were alone for a month or so, we could really get to know one another.'

She knew she ought to say yes. She knew Alex was making an effort, suggesting something very sensible. If only she could talk to him honestly! At that moment she cursed her own ability to hide her emotions, her inability to reveal what she felt in her heart of hearts. But she had never done that with anyone. Not even Charles. She was so well practised at hiding her disappointments, coping alone with her problems that now, when she wanted desperately to change her ways, she found she could not.

Besides, while she had spent the entire day trying to convince herself that the goings-on between Alex and Stella were not really her business, she was forced to admit there was another reason why she couldn't broach the subject with Alex: she might hear something she didn't want to hear.

As things stood, her relationship with Alex was holding together. The threads were thin, but they were there. On a surface level, at least, they were getting on well. For the time being she wanted everything to stay just as it was—

in every way. That she was going through a period of adjustment was clear even to herself. Her emotions were frozen, catatonic, and until she had sorted them out, she didn't want to rock the boat in either direction. She was afraid to.

Her voice, therefore, was as casual and reasonable as she could make it when she gave Alex his answer. 'Personally, I'd rather stay here. I love this house, the peacefulness. And—and I honestly think that for the time being it's good that we're not spending all day together.'

He reached for a cigarette, his puzzled look making her feel obliged to go on. 'You see, I—we're both sort of adjusting to a new situation and I feel ... I think ...' Her voice trailed away because he was looking at her so intently. His very nearness was making her nervous.

As if sensing how she felt, Alex moved away from her. He strode over to the bar and refilled his glass. The distance between them gave Gina new courage, and since he obviously still didn't know what she was trying to convey, she tried a different tack.

'We did agree—before we entered into this marriage—that I could have freedom. I mean, what I mean is——' It was coming out wrong! That wasn't how she'd meant to put it ...

'I see.'

'No! Alex, what I mean is——'

'What you mean is that I'm crowding you.' There was an odd note in his voice, but it wasn't one of annoyance. 'I'm sorry, Gina. And you're absolutely right. You must be your own person. I did promise you all the freedom you wanted.'

Gina lifted her glass to her lips, drank its entire content in one go. It didn't help. It didn't help her feel less tense. Oh, if only she could tell Alex how she *really* felt! If she could at least find the right words to help her over this moment.

But Alex found them for her. 'What you're really saying

is that you want things to stay just as they are.' It was not a question, it was a statement.

'Y-yes.'

'In every respect?' That was a question—a loaded question.

'Yes, Alex. In every respect.'

They were living on borrowed time. Gina knew that as well as Alex surely must have known it. Three whole weeks slipped by—astonishingly quickly. Gina was surprised how easily she filled her time. But there was always something to do, and not for an instant did she get bored.

She made breakfast herself. After that she would take a walk or drive the sports car into Nairobi and do some shopping. There, she had bought an easel, paints and brushes. She had started her painting of the *shamba*, the hills, and had spent most of her afternoons sitting, painting, on the first floor balcony, where she could get a better perspective of the landscape.

A pattern had taken shape in their lives, and while it was far from ideal, it was at least fairly satisfactory. For the time being. There was no strain between herself and Alex, nor was there any closeness. There was never a shortage of something to talk about, but their conversations never veered onto dangerous ground.

She knew it couldn't last, of course. Alex's toothbrush was no longer on the shelf in the master bathroom. His clothes were no longer in the wardrobe. Alex had removed them, but he had made no comment about it. It had been an enormous relief to Gina, and she loved him for it; for his patience, for not putting pressure on her. Indeed that was the one thing which did not remain static: her love for him.

As each day unfolded she loved him more and more, regardless of all she didn't know about him. What she did know was enough to make her love him—the kindly way he treated old Kimau, who looked at Alex as if he were a god. The discipline and respect he evoked from his workers, the way he was master of his home and all he surveyed. The way he never failed to appreciate the little things, the flowers Gina kept in every room, the meals she arranged or cooked for him. The way he frequently asked her out, almost as if he were trying to ensure she didn't become bored. The look on his face as they sat quietly together listening to the music of their favourite composer.

It was heartbreaking for Gina to realise that one kiss, just one kiss, could so easily be the start of that which would break down most of the barriers between them. But she was terrified to light that particular touchpaper, unable to be intimate with a man who did not love her, a man who thought she had got married because she had nothing better to do, a man who had married her in order to have a companion, a resident housekeeper and hostess.

Gina was frightened by her frigidity. More than once it had occurred to her that if she were in this situation in London, she could go to a sexologist. Maybe there was someone here, in Nairobi. Maybe there was a doctor, a counsellor ... But what would she tell such a person? That she was frigid, had a mental block? That she lay in bed night after night yearning to feel her husband's arms around her, his lips, his body on hers? That she longed for this—but turned to ice when he came within three feet of her?

No, it couldn't last. If Gina put it into the crudest terms, Alex was keeping his side of their bargain—while she was breaking hers. Viewing the situation in a more basic, practical light, she could not escape from the fact that Alex was a passionate, red-blooded man and very, very soon something would have to give. His patience would not last for ever.

Gina was not surprised, then, when everything came to a head at the beginning of their fourth week together. She wasn't surprised, but she was shattered, totally annihilated by the outcome. It was a Sunday. They were lounging by the swimming pool in an afternoon that was perfect in its warmth, tranquillity and stillness.

Gina was dressed in a bikini, a little lemon affair made from cotton. Her eyes were closed, her head turned away from her husband as she spoke to him. 'Heavens, I forgot to tell you that Daddy phoned yesterday.'

'Yes?' Alex said lazily. 'How is the old devil?'

'Fine! Really well. Or so he says ... anyhow, we'll have the chance to find out for ourselves next week. Tomorrow they're moving into their house. The furniture's already gone down by road. They're giving their housewarming party on Saturday, this coming Saturday.'

'Wow!' She could hear the smile in Alex's voice. 'I hadn't realised how long it's been ... I must ring Stella and ask if there's anything she needs. We'd better think about a gift, too.'

Stella. Why did she have to be his first consideration?

'I—I have a gift for them.'

She could sense that his eyes were upon her. 'You have? What is it? When did you shop for it?'

'I—I'll show it to you later,' she mumbled, wishing for the impossible. That she could refuse to go to her father's housewarming party. She would hate seeing Alex and Stella together. She would hate having to face all the doubts and misgivings she was managing currently to push to the back of her mind. She would hate having to pretend, to pretend to her stepmother that everything was just fine with the marriage she'd warned Gina against. But she would do it. She would do it if it killed her.

Alex's sudden silence got to her then, puzzled her. In an effort to see what he was thinking, she turned over on to her back. It was then that the whole world tilted sideways. His eyes were travelling slowly over the two scanty pieces of cotton which were hiding her nakedness. As his gaze locked with hers she saw pure desire reflected in his eyes. Incredibly, unbelievably Gina realised it was a reflection of what she, too, was feeling. Within those few seconds there flared between them that overwhelming, almost indescribable magnetism which had consumed them both on the dance-floor of a Nairobi nightclub a long, long time ago. The air between them was charged electrically with pure, unadulterated physical lust.

Alex's voice was hardly more than a groan as he spoke her name. But even as his arms reached for her, her body stiffened, her hands tightening into fists as she gripped frantically against the mattress she was lying on. She couldn't move, couldn't speak. She knew nothing but a voice screaming inside her head: 'No! Don't, don't!' and a ghastly confusion as she realised it was a command both to herself and to her husband. She was screaming at herself not to freeze; to relax, relax ... and it was also a silent plea for Alex not to come any closer.

But Alex had frozen, too. He was sitting on the edge of his sun-lounger, rigid with anger. Gina closed her eyes against the glare of his, seeing that the passion and yearning so recently burning there had been replaced by something she couldn't bring herself to name.

Terror choked off her breath as she braced herself for the explosion. The volcano was erupting. The time-bomb she'd been living with for almost a month ...

He didn't shout. He didn't move. But every carefully chosen word he spoke cut through her like a knife. 'You needn't look so petrified. I will not demand even from my wife that which she is not prepared to give. To *give*! But that's a word you don't know the meaning of. Hell, I'm not just talking about your body—I mean everything! I've had it, Gina! You feel you were bulldozed into this marriage—this *institution*, as you once called it—and you've spent the past three weeks regretting it.'

'Alex, please——' It was difficult even to push two words past the restriction in her throat.

'Alex, please!' He stood, glaring down at her as he flung her words back in her face. 'Alex, please ... I'm sick of hearing that every time I reach for your hand across the dining table, every time we come close together in the swimming pool. In fact, any time I get within a yard of you!

'I've had it! Isn't that a tremendous relief to you? Is it plain enough? You've made it very clear what you want, and I'm in full agreement with you! I'll see my lawyer tomorrow. We'll get this marriage annulled in less time than it took to enter into it!'

He stalked away from her, leaving her stupefied, terrified, a trembling mass of raw emotion. 'Alex!' The cry tore from her throat as she leapt to her feet, stunned into action as the finality of his words permeated her brain.

She started after him, but he had almost reached the house, and coming round the corner of the house, hurrying towards him was a long-legged blonde, her features breaking into a smile as she came to a halt.

Everything went blurred, the whole world seemed to shift on its axis as the blood pounded in Gina's ears and she cursed Mandy Miller to hell and damnation.

Alex's arm slipped around Mandy's waist in a gesture that was oh, so painfully familiar! He bent, whispering something into her ear. Gina stood motionless, humiliated. Had he told Mandy the truth? Heavens, had he just told that scheming vulture of the decision he'd reached?

She walked towards them, forcing herself not to break into a run. As she walked past them into the house she was unable to look at Alex, was compelled to try and read Mandy Miller's eyes. She wished she hadn't. Mandy looked smug, triumphant, as a knowing smile hovered around her over-painted lips.

When the other girl spoke, Gina averted her head. 'Excuse me.' That was all she managed to say, though it was far from all she wanted to say. There was the tinkle of Mandy's laughter and the sentence, spoken loudly so it would reach Gina's ears: 'Alex darling, it looks as if I've picked the wrong moment to come visiting!'

From the sanctuary of her first-floor bedroom, Gina looked down towards the swimming pool. She didn't cry.

She didn't even try to sort things out in her mind. It was too late for that. Much too late.

Mandy Miller was sitting on the lounger Gina had been sitting on. It seemed ironically appropriate that she should do so. Gina watched her as she sat chatting to Alex. Chatting, flirting . . . tempting. The wretched woman had been hanging around like a vulture waiting to pounce. Twice a week she had called at the house, watching, quizzing, waiting to walk right into Gina's shoes. She had been after Alex Craig for a long time. Well, this was her big chance. Gina had blown her chance. It was over between her and Alex, and Mandy Miller was there with him now.

Like one who was mesmerized Gina watched what was happening. From the chaos of her mind there surfaced only one thought: if a man doesn't get fed at home, he'll go and eat in a restaurant. Crude, perhaps, but true.

Mandy was tugging at Alex's arm, and he stood, smiling as he picked up his shirt, slipped into his shoes. Wearing flesh-coloured stretch pants and something resembling a bikini top, Mandy Miller had put on display that which she was obviously willing to give. To *give*. Her full breasts were straining against the material of her top, young and full—and no doubt irresistible to a man who had been on a starvation diet.

Yes, Gina was bitter. But she could see only the raw facts. At last, a little realism had crept into her thinking. She had to face facts. She saw black and she saw white, and if there were any shades in between, she was certainly blind to them then.

As Alex and Mandy walked away from the house, Gina resigned herself to the inevitable. She had lost Alex Craig as surely as if she herself had insisted on the annulment.

Within minutes she heard the sound of a car engine being kicked into motion, and then the fading hum as Alex and Mandy drove away from the *shamba*. Gina lay down on the bed and stared, unblinkingly, at the ceiling.

CHAPTER NINE

On her lap there was a very old, very battered book which taught the rudiments of Swahili. It was open, but Gina wasn't looking at it. She had found it in the library and unbeknown to Alex she had been studying it each evening in bed. Or in the middle of the night. Or in the early hours of the morning. In between short stretches of fitful sleep. She had intended to surprise Alex with her new-found knowledge—as soon as she could string a few sentences together.

Now, there was no point in studying further. No point in anything at all. Her eyes flitted restlessly around the garden, the most beautiful part of the entire *shamba*. Gina had come here in the hope that its peace and tranquillity would communicate itself to her. It had failed in that respect, though its omnipresent beauty never failed to please her eye.

At the bottom of the garden a complex matting of creepers pushed their way across the wall. In front of the wall were the avocado trees, heavily laden with their lush fruits. Closer to her were hibiscus and oleander and the myriad scarlet bells which cascaded from the branches of the Australian flames, her favourites. From her seat beneath the makuruwe tree the heady scent of frangipani reached her nostrils.

Gina breathed deeply, drinking in the beauty and the scent of the garden, trying to steady her nerves, and knowing she would soon be leaving this place which had so quickly become home to her.

Alex hadn't returned last night, at least, not before Gina had retired to her room. She had listened intently for the sound of his car, but had heard nothing. It was possible he'd come home, that the size of the big old house had obscured any noise. It didn't matter. Mandy Miller had needed only a couple of hours with him to achieve what she had wanted to achieve.

'*Jambo, memsab.*' Gina started at the sound of Kimau's voice close by. She smiled at him, and he smiled back, but the kindly old eyes seemed troubled today. Or was it just her imagination?

'Bwana is on the telephone. He is asking for you, *memsab.*'

Gina bolted towards the house in an ungainly fashion, leaving Kimau to amble his way back in his slow but graceful gait. When she picked up the receiver her legs turned to water and she sank on to a nearby chair, her hands holding so tightly to the instrument that the whites of her knuckles were showing.

'Alex?'

'Gina, I'm in town.' His voice was crisp, clear, distant. 'I'm ringing to let you know that I have to go down to Mombasa. They're having a few problems at the factory.'

'I . . . see.' Oh, dear God, she prayed, please help me. Don't let me say the wrong thing. 'How . . . how long will you be away? I mean, will you be back in time for Daddy's party?'

'Of course. I'll be back on Wednesday. You don't think I'd let Stella down, do you?'

No, of course he wouldn't let Stella down. But oh, the irony! In the final analysis it was not Stella who was the enemy. It was Alex's ex-girl-friend, Mandy Miller. And this trip to Mombasa just had to be an excuse for a few days away with her. . . .

Gina swallowed hard as her stomach lurched, the moisture in her mouth turning acid. 'Have you . . .' *Have you spoken to your lawyer?* was what she wanted to say.

'What?' His voice was tinged with impatience.

'Have you . . . have you got some spare clothes with you? I mean, are you coming home——'

'I took everything I need when I left this morning. I'm leaving now, in fact. Goodbye, Gina.'

He hung up before she could say anything else.

She sat staring stupidly at the telephone. He was taking Mandy away with him. It had to be! The timing . . . it was just too much of a coincidence that there were really problems at the factory. Wednesday—that would give him three whole days and two more nights with Mandy Miller.

There comes a point when you have to concede defeat. That thought didn't take long to register with Gina, after the numbness began to fade. She stayed in the same room, in the same chair, by the telephone. She still hadn't fully absorbed all the shock—of the annulment, of Alex's affair with Mandy Miller, but she had adjusted to it sufficiently for the numbness to lift. And then the pain set in. Like the post-operative pain that makes itself known when the anaesthetic wears off. The only difference was that this pain would never fade, never heal.

Nobody could help her now. It was too late. Oh, why hadn't she cut her losses, got out of Africa as soon as she started falling for Alex? She smiled wryly to herself as she thought of the answer: because falling in love with Alex Craig had been an insidious process, something that had started long before she realised how much she loved him.

How naïve she had been! How stupid and naïve. Her youth was the only excuse for that. How stupid even to think their marriage stood a chance, how stupid she had been to think she could make Alex love her. Maybe there would have been a hope of that if . . . but how could she have anticipated this terrifying frigidity that had taken control of her? How could she have anticipated how awful it would be to live with a man, loving him desperately— and knowing he didn't love her?

Stella had been right. Despite Harry's shrewdness, as a woman Stella had had far more insight . . .

In the early hours of Tuesday morning, Gina woke to

find Stella's name on her lips. Thoughts of her stepmother still rankled. While there was nothing whatever Gina could do about Mandy Miller, there was some unfinished business with Stella which she intended to clear up before she left Africa.

Not for a moment did Gina think it would do any good. It was purely a matter of pride, of principle. What little pride Gina had left was dictating that she let Stella know she was not a total fool, that she was aware of the secret business between her and Alex; that she was also aware of the influence she had over Alex—an influence that went far deeper than the ability to lend or give away money.

And Stella had used that influence to Gina's detriment. Hadn't her phone call on the wedding night been a largely contributing factor to Gina's withdrawal from her husband? That, plus the fact that she had told Alex yet again what a mistake he'd made.

How many times had she told him since then? How many times had she repeated her opinion in numerous phone calls over the past three weeks? Gina wasn't seeking to deny her own mistakes, to place all the blame for her failure elsewhere. But *some* blame was attributable to her stepmother, and if for no other reason than that, she intended to give Stella a piece of her mind.

When she found herself still thinking in the same vein on Wednesday, Gina was convinced of the rightness of her decision. Stella had to be told. There was someone else who would be given the sharp edge of Gina's tongue, too . . . if she had the audacity again to set foot on these premises before Gina had vacated them. No, come to think of it, a hard slap across the face would be more fitting for the likes of Mandy Miller.

It helped, the return of her pugnacity and the aggression which had once been so much a part of her personality. Facets of her character which Alex had criticised so heartily in the early days. He had been right, too. They were protective barriers, defence mechanisms she had used to protect herself from all sorts of hurts. Well, they were firmly in place again now, and she needed them as she had never needed them before.

Alex sensed the change in her as soon as he walked through the door in the early evening. She knew it, she knew he disapproved of it. But what the hell difference did it make now?

There was something different about Alex, too. For the first time ever it seemed he had been unable to shed his temper—despite the distractions which had engaged him for the past three days. He wasn't overtly angry. In fact, that would have been easier to handle. Rather it was as if he had switched Gina off completely. She was there, he talked to her politely if sparsely, but somewhere deep inside him there was a coldness which reflected in his attitude, his eyes, his voice—even the way he moved. He was tense, and that was something which had been totally alien to him before.

'You were going to show me the housewarming gift for Harry and Stella.' He was already on his third cigarette after dinner—something else which was different about him.

'Yes. I—it would be easier if you'd come into the library with me. It's in there. I—it's a little heavy to——' Oh dear, it was difficult, coping with him now. It was like living on a knife's edge. She could hardly bear to look at him, so strong was the tension between them.

The painting of the *shamba* was lying on the huge, leather-topped desk in the library. Gina lifted the dust cover and stepped back, hoping Alex would consider it good enough to give as a present.

He said nothing for a long moment, concentrating on the painting as if the view it depicted were unfamiliar to him. 'It's brilliant,' he said at length.

A nervous laugh escaped her. 'You don't have to say that, Alex. Just tell me whether it's good enough to give——'

'I'm not giving this away, I'm keeping it. That is, if you don't mind?'

'No, of course I wouldn't mind. But it seems so silly when you've got the reality of the view right outside your window.'

He turned to her then, some sort of emotion flitting across the depths of his eyes, albeit something unidentifiable. 'Why *did* you quit art school, Gina?'

The question threw her. 'Because—because I wasn't talented enough to—I wasn't good enough.'

A smile pulled at the corners of his lips as his eyes went back to the painting. 'I don't believe that. I recognise what's good when I see it. But far be it from me to delve into your private thoughts and reasoning.'

She stiffened. She realised he was criticising her, but she didn't really understand what he meant. And why did he want to keep the painting himself? Was he being kind? No, not now. He'd gone past that stage. Maybe it was just a way of ensuring that Stella and Harry were given something else. Maybe he didn't honestly think the painting good enough, after all. But that didn't ring true, either. Alex Craig was blunt enough to tell her, if he thought it was rubbish. So perhaps . . . for a moment a foolish little hope trembled through her . . . perhaps he wanted to keep it as a memento, a reminder of her? And if that were the case, he must feel something for her. Something, however little . . .

'Alex.' She asserted herself, squaring her shoulders and forcing her eyes to meet with his, her voice as emotionless as she could make it. 'Alex, I'd like to know what's happening. I have to sort myself out. Did you see your lawyer?'

He looked at her briefly, coldly, before walking over to the window, his hands thrust deep inside his trouser pockets as he kept his back to her. 'There wasn't time on Monday. I had to take off for Mombasa, remember? I'll see him next Monday. Which reminds me . . .'

So he hadn't had second thoughts. Far from it. Gina's heart plummeted and she inwardly cursed her stupidity for daring to nurture just a little bit of hope. Would she ever learn? The only thing which had prevented Alex from setting the annulment procedure into motion had been his eagerness to get into bed with Mandy Miller. And in all the circumstances, Gina couldn't honestly blame the man for that.

'. . . About this weekend. We can tell your parents then.' Gina looked at him helplessly. The idea of telling her father what was happening filled her with dread. But it had to be done.

Her nervousness went unnoticed. Alex still had his back to her. 'I'll do the talking, if you'd prefer. It'll have to wait until Sunday, in any case. We don't want to spoil the housewarming party. We'll ask them over to the bungalow for lunch on Sunday, and tell them then.'

'Alex, my boy! Where the hell've you been? I was about to send out a search party. The party's been under way for over an hour!' Such was Harry Duncan's boisterous greeting as Alex and Gina slipped into their lounge. Already Gina could see her stepmother gravitating towards them, cutting a graceful path through the occupants of the room.

'Sorry, Harry,' Alex grinned. 'We got to the bungalow a little late. Last-minute business, you know . . .'

'I understand! Georgina dear, you look——' Her father stood back and appraised her, as if unsure how she looked. 'Very—grown-up, I suppose. Yes, marriage has been good for you. I can see that without looking.'

Gina smiled at him, watching the big brown eyes which were so much like her own. If her father really meant what he'd said, her smile and her appearance must be giving entirely the wrong impression. So far, so good. That was just the impression Gina wanted to give. Tomorrow would be the time for a showdown—for truth.

'Gina dear, you look super! So . . . sophisticated!' Stella smiled her most charming smile, and Gina forced herself to reciprocate. Actually, her dress wasn't unlike Stella's, except that Gina's was black while her stepmother's was turquoise. It was a straight, simple little number with a deep V in the front and a very low back. It was sleeveless, nicely set off by a plain black choker, and yes, she was aware that she looked sophisticated. Or grown-up, as her father had put it!

'Thank you, Stella. You're looking very well, too.' Gina just managed to get in the required response before Stella's attention turned to Alex and the fussing and compliment-ing started all over again.

There followed a horrible moment which Gina did not see coming, and was helpless to prevent.

'Everyone! Everybody—may I have your attention for a moment?' Harry's gruff voice boomed across the room, his glass raised high in the air as he smiled broadly at the forty or more people who were present. Curious eyes moved towards the small group by the doorway. Someone turned down the music. Mouths were smiling, chatter was dying away as everyone gave their attention to Harry.

'Our last guests have arrived!' he boomed. 'And since we all know one another—it's probably quicker to intro-duce this couple to you all at the same time!'

Gina shot him a sideways look, her stomach forming a knot as she realised what was coming. Had Harry been drinking? Of course he had! So had everyone else! He'd obviously had enough already—as much if not more than his health dictated . . .

'This is my daughter Georgina.' He bowed slightly, his arm sweeping out in a gesture of introduction as Gina bit her tongue and put on her brightest smile. Damn Harry! He never used to be like this!

'And this is Alex Craig—her husband! These youngsters got married only a month ago—and I'd like to propose a toast to the happy couple!'

It was horrible. But there was no use in wishing the floor would open up and swallow her, when she knew damn well it wouldn't. A sea of faces was smiling at her, congratulations, laughter and teasing little comments bandied about the room, before someone turned up the music to a louder pitch than it had been before, and the party continued.

With a surreptitious glance at her husband Gina saw that he, at least, had been true to himself. Alex wasn't smiling.

Within two minutes Gina was standing among a group of five people, ensconced in a conversation which featured herself, her marriage and her home for the first, awful ten minutes.

'Well, how do you like being married?'

'Ah, you've done it now! Too late, too late was the cry!'

'Oh, shut up, Henry! Stop teasing. Tell me, dear, how do you like living on such a vast plantation? I hear Alex Craig owns one of the biggest——'

'Your husband must be very busy at the moment, what with the crops being harvested——'

'You got married in Malindi? How quaint——'

'Where did you go for your honeymoon?'

'How do you like living in Africa?'

'Do you plan to start a family soon?'

'Henry!'

'Alice dear, it's a reasonable question! What do you say, Georgina? I'll bet old Harry's looking forward to having grandchildren——'

How Gina coped with it, she would never know. It wasn't until she had finished her second Campari and soda that she began to relax. By the time she was halfway through her third her thoughts became positively perverse. Perhaps she should put an end to this sham right now. Stand on a table and make an announcement—tell everyone present that her marriage had been a farce. That it was about to be terminated, annulled, cancelled out as if it had never taken place.

Of course she did no such thing. Like the polite, refined young woman she was supposed to be, she played the role of Alex Craig's wife, and Harry Duncan's daughter, to perfection. But all the time she was acting, chatting, circulating, the periphery of her vision monitored the only two people in the room who really interested her. Stella had not monopolised Alex. She was flitting about like the perfect hostess she was, ensuring that her guests' glasses were kept full, inviting them to eat from the buffet, chatting, charming, laughing.

Alex was in the far corner of the room, diagonally across from her. He was silent, listening with apparent interest to a big, burly man who was talking his head off, making wide, sweeping gestures with the hand that wasn't holding a glass, shrugging hefty shoulders every now and then.

Gina had to force herself not to stare. Alex looked so beautiful, resplendent in a white suit and an open-necked black shirt which set off the depth of his tan. Even from a distance the outstanding blueness of his eyes could be seen, the straight, aristocratic nose, the firm, sensuous mouth . . .

Gina closed her eyes, trying to block out the vision of the face she loved so dearly. The face she had not yet drawn. Perhaps it was just as well. She would be taking no sketches, no mementoes back to England with her. She had to forget, forget . . .

Her fourth drink made her positively depressed. She wouldn't be able to stand this scene much longer, not without bursting into tears and making a complete fool of herself. And she couldn't afford to do that. Not when there was unfinished business to be dealt with.

Gina's gaze came to rest on her stepmother, signalling that she was about to leave the room, that she wanted Stella to follow her. She saw the worried look in the older woman's eyes, the frown pulling at her delicately-shaped brows. And then she nodded, letting Gina know she'd got the message.

Stella followed immediately, taking Gina's arm as she came face to face with her on the upstairs landing. 'Darling, what is it?'

Gina shook off her hand. 'I want to talk to you, Stella. I appreciate that we're in the middle of a party, but it's important.'

'Of course, of course! Come into our bedroom, dear. We won't be disturbed there.'

Stella sat on the edge of the bed, her hands clenched together in her lap as Gina remained standing, her arms folded across her waist.

Gina got directly to the point, plunging straight into speech before the very pointlessness of what she was doing made her lose courage. 'Stella, there's something going on between you and my husband. I'd like to know what it is.'

'Something . . .? My dear, there's nothing . . . I don't know what you mean. What are you talking about?'

It was a moment Gina would never forget. If she didn't know for a fact that Stella was lying, she'd have been tempted to believe her. The expression on her step-mother's face was one of incredulity.

'Something *underhand*, Stella.' Gina's voice was an angry hiss. 'Something you've been trying to keep secret. Something to do with money. That—among other things. So don't lie to me. I'm aware that you and Alex are up to something, and I want to know about it. I want you to be the one who tells me. Now!'

It was a few seconds before Stella reacted, then her face went pale, but even as that happened, her body seemed to relax. 'Oh, dear lord, is that it? You mean, Alex hasn't told you? Oh, really! Oh, the *idiot*. I told him, begged of him to explain everything to you——'

Gina was getting more impatient by the minute. She wasn't fooled by this—this actress! 'Stop playing for time!

I don't want a bunch of lies. Get on with it!'

Stella floundered, her head moving from side to side as if she couldn't believe what was happening. 'Sit down, Gina,' she said at length. 'I'll explain it to you—since Alex obviously hasn't. It—it's not very nice, so I'd prefer you to sit.'

'I can take it,' Gina snapped. 'Don't concern yourself with me. I'm way past the capacity for being shocked. Way past it.'

'As you wish ... My dear, there's been a—a transaction—between myself and Alex. I—it became necessary to——— Oh, dear, I'd better start at the beginning ...

'While Harry and I were away there was a phone call from Mr Ngara. In fact, I believe you took the call yourself. Mr Ngara is—was—the site manager on your father's copper mine. You—you know about the mine, don't you? Well, Mr Ngara was a total incompetent. He was supposed to be a good man, he'd been recommended as a man who knew what he was doing. Gina, I honestly don't understand the technicalities, but it seems that during the excavations they'd come across a hitch—a thick belt of rock which hadn't been accounted for. Ngara had approached things the wrong way, it seems.'

She shrugged, looking helplessly at Gina, her eyes pleading for the younger woman to understand. 'Darling, the upshot was that we had to plough a lot more money into the mine. Money that your father didn't have ...'

As the picture began to unfold, Gina slumped against the wall. She could almost guess what was coming next.

'... Alex talked to Mr Ngara that day you went to Nairobi. He fired him there and then. Not that it solved much. The fact remained that in order to reach pay dirt more work than was anticipated had to be done on the mine—and that meant more money.'

The tables turned. Stella got up, moved around the room restlessly as Gina slumped into a chair, feeling as if she were drowning. Feeling foolish, sorry—and angry because her own husband hadn't been bothered to explain all this to her! Why? Why the hell hadn't he told her? There had to be more to it . . .

'Alex has a small share in the mine. Very small. He'd have invested more with Harry, but he was having the old cash-flow problem. He'd bought this factory in Mombasa, you see, bought it as a going concern. So at the time of the distribution of shares, Alex took just a nominal amount. Your father is virtually the sole shareholder, owning ninety-five per cent.

'Gina, Harry's sunk everything he's got into that mine. Everything! And there's a further hundred thousand pounds' worth of work to be done. So I put up the money. I didn't dare tell your father—I couldn't! Not then, not when he was feeling so ill and his brother had just died——'

'Oh, God!' Gina was disgusted. With Alex, with Stella, but mostly with herself. 'Does Daddy know what you've done? Have you told him now?'

'No!' Stella was instantly alarmed. 'I don't see the need. I mean, I—why do we need to tell him? Gina, you know how proud he is! He'd hate the idea of my bailing him out, even though that might sound incredibly stupid. It's just his way. I—I see no need to tell him. He'd be so cross, so upset. He—I—Alex and I thought it would be——'

Gina held up her hand, sighing wearily at the stupidity of it all, the unnecessary worry this had caused her, the misunderstandings. But how on earth could she be cross with Stella now? Over this business, at least, she couldn't possibly remain angry.

'Calm down, Stella. I understand. You and Alex decided between you not to tell Daddy. You were terrified of bringing on a heart attack, or something. You raised the money—which explains your "shopping" trip into Nairobi. You and Alex went to the bank. It took a while to sort things out. On our wedding day, when we gave you a lift to Nairobi, you slipped away from Daddy for a while and completed your transactions, transferred your money into Alex's account so that *he* could put it into the mine—thus keeping your name out of it.'

Stella nodded, frowning. 'That's right. I had to order money from America. But how come you know that much, when you didn't know——'

'Because I overheard Alex talking to you. I was on the balcony outside our bedroom. I could hear every word he spoke, and I gleaned that much. I also——' Gina re-asserted herself. There was something else which had to be cleared up. 'I also heard him admitting to you that he might have made a mistake. You must have been telling him he'd been a fool to marry me.'

Stella was shaking her head sadly. 'You don't think much of me, do you, Gina? You're wrong. I was telling him then that he should confide in you, that it would be a mistake not to. Even before you were married, I'd told Alex that we should let you know what we'd done for Harry. But Alex said no, you had a lot on your mind. He said he didn't want to worry you in any way. He said he'd tell you all about it after you'd settled down with him.'

'Well, he didn't!' Gina said bitterly. 'Alex tells me nothing! He came upstairs that night and lied to me—he said the phone call was an overseas business call. Can you imagine what went through my mind, Stella? Can you?'

There was a long silence during which Stella kept her eyes fixed on Gina's face. Gina squirmed uncomfortably. 'I'm sorry, Stella. I—I'd made all the wrong guesses. I— I'm sorry for attacking you. I thought you'd been influencing Alex . . .'

Stella patted the bed. 'Come and sit beside me, Gina. Please, let me help you.'

'Help me?' Gina's head shot up proudly. 'We have nothing more to say. I've apologised. You—you'd better get back to the party.'

'Blow the party. Darling, can't we be friends? Won't you confide in me?'

'There's nothing to confide.' The kindness in Stella's voice was getting to her. Gina could feel tears threatening. She'd been wrong about her stepmother, time and time again.

'Gina, I've been watching you this evening—all that false gaiety and laughter, and two things are quite obvious to me: you're deeply in love with Alex, and something is very, very wrong with your marriage.'

'We're splitting.' The words came bitterly, unthinkingly. But what did it matter? Everything would be out in the open tomorrow, in any case. What was the use of perpetuating this pretence? 'You were right, Stella—our marriage was doomed from the start.'

'No! I was wrong.' Stella spoke slowly, separating each word as if she couldn't emphasise them enough. 'I said a marriage without love is doomed. I was concerned for *you*. You're so young, I didn't want you rushing—but I didn't realise then that you were in love with Alex. As a woman, I should have seen that. But I was too distracted with the mine business, too worried about Harry——'

Gina looked up then, all the respect she felt for the older woman unmistakable in her eyes. Stella Duncan was really rather special. Maybe . . . perhaps she could confide in her? But thinking that and doing it were two different things. Old habits die hard, and Gina found it virtually impossible to say what was in her heart.

'Gina, you say you're splitting. I can't believe—I mean, haven't you told Alex how you feel about him? No? But, my dear, that's so silly!' Stella's voice hardened as she crossed over to where Gina was sitting. 'I once told you that the best way for us to become friends was for me to speak my mind. It cuts both ways, you know. And it applies in marriage, too. How can you and Alex even get started when you don't communicate with each other? Tell him how you feel! Gina, one of your worst failings is this enormous ability you have to keep your thoughts and feelings to yourself. Oh, you're quick with your sarcasm, and there's always a witty or a cutting retort, but it's not *honest*. It isn't really you. Even your father doesn't know you well! You leave everyone guessing as to what your real feelings are. If you understood Alex better, you'd see that it's——'

'I can't!' The words came from between clenched teeth; Gina was fighting desperately to hold back her tears. As Stella knelt beside her, reaching for her hand, she recoiled. 'I'm not going to make a fool of myself with Alex. He doesn't love me—he feels nothing! If he's able to love anyone, Stella, it's you!'

For a fleeting moment there was a look of horror stamped on her stepmother's face. Then, amazingly, she was laughing. 'Oh, Gina, Gina! Don't you know *anything* about Alex? Hasn't he told you anything? Dear lord, how can you live with someone for a whole month and not begin to understand them just a little bit? Of course he loves me—but not in the way you mean! He feels protective towards me. Can't you see that?'

She'd lost Gina now. She looked at her dubiously, seeing that Stella was exasperated yet tremendously patient at the same time. 'Let me tell you a few things about that husband of yours,' Stella went on. 'If he likes someone, he likes them regardless of what they do. If he loves—he loves for ever. He loves me. Ever since I left Kenya, he's kept in touch, taken an interest in what I've been doing. He even came to America from time to time. He cares so much *because I'm his sister-in-law*. I was married to his older brother. Alex worshipped David. David was twelve years his senior and could do no wrong in his younger brother's eyes. That's normal enough ... and because David had chosen me, Alex thought I must be wonderful! He still thinks I am.

'But there's more to it. I'm the only surviving member of his family, and that in itself means a lot to Alex. You see, he lost his brother when he was nineteen. When he was eighteen, his father died. A year before that, his mother died from cancer . . . Do you begin to understand, Gina?'

'I—think so.' The tears had started. Just a small crack in the dam that had been built upon and reinforced over so many weeks. When Stella put her arms around her, Gina didn't protest. The gesture made the tears flow more readily and with that came a glimmer of real hope. If she could talk to Alex, really communicate with him . . .

As if reading her mind, Stella voiced the thought. 'Talk to him! For heaven's sake, Gina, get to know one another. Don't give up. Don't tell me you're splitting when this can so easily be remedied!'

Easily? If only she knew! If only she knew about Mandy Miller, about Gina's frigidity. How closely those two were connected . . . without the frigidity, Alex would not have got involved with Mandy. She was certain of that; he felt nothing for the girl. It was just sex.

'Stella, you don't understand. You've been very sweet to me, and I appreciate it. I—but it's over between me and Alex. It's what he wants. And—and there's this big probl——' Oh, how could she say it? How could she risk being laughed at?

Stella's arms tightened around her. 'You mean, Alex has actually spoken about splitting? I'd thought—I'd thought it was just your idea. I didn't think Alex . . . You mean he wants it, too? He's actually told you he wants a divorce?'

'Not a divorce. An *annulment*!' It was the best Gina could do, the only way she could even broach the subject. Then the dam burst and she was sobbing, her body trembling, racked with emotion as she finally gave vent to the tears she had withheld for so many weeks.

But Stella wasn't laughing. Nor was she shocked. She just held tightly to her stepdaughter until the tears began to subside. 'I might've guessed,' she said softly. 'But that's a minor problem. You've got to bear in mind——'

'*Minor?* Stella, how can you say that?' Stella's accept-ance, her casualness had given Gina the courage to go on, though she couldn't understand Stella's reasoning.

But Harry Duncan chose that precise moment to put his head round the door. 'What's going on here? Stella, I've been——'

Stella shot to the door in the space of three seconds. 'Darling! I'll only be a moment. Gina and I were having a little talk.'

Gina turned her head away from the light, grateful that Stella had prevented Harry from entering the room.

'What's with those two?' Harry Duncan made no attempt to lower his voice. 'They haven't even spoken to each other all evening!'

'But that's how it is at parties. People are supposed to circulate!'

'Stella——' Gina cringed at the note of warning in her father's voice.

'Oh, don't be such a busybody,' Stella said lightly. 'They've had a bit of a row, that's all. Gina and I are just indulging in girl-talk. I'm . . . giving her a few hints.'

Gina could only guess at the expression Stella must have worn on her face when she said that. Or perhaps the wink she'd given to her husband. Whatever—it worked. Harry chuckled, accepted the explanation. In fact, he was probably only too pleased that Gina and his wife had become close enough to talk at such a level. He went away happily enough.

'Stella . . .?'

'Yes, I said it was minor, and I meant it. It'll happen when the time is right. As it does in all relationships—inside or outside of marriage.'

'No, you still don't understand.' Gina's voice dropped to a whisper. 'Stella, I—I've become fr-frigid!'

'Rubbish!' Stella smiled at the look on her face. 'Few women can jump into bed with a man and be content to get to know him after that's happened. There are some who're made that way, but for most of us it's necessary for emotions to be involved first. Now, you're deeply in love with Alex—but you've no idea what he feels for you. Darling, you're not frigid, you're simply insecure. Don't you see that?'

It wasn't an entirely new thought to Gina, of course. But it did help, hearing her stepmother reach the same conclusion. It reassured her that she wasn't in some way abnormal, that perhaps this thing was more common in women than she had thought it was. But where did she go from here? 'It—it shouldn't be happening now we've been married for a month, though, should it?'

Stella smiled sadly. 'Darling, I really can't help you any further. It's up to you now. You and Alex. I know what you need, but I can't speak for him. Tonight is the first time I've seen him since your marriage; he hasn't confided in me. I don't know what he feels for you. But bear in mind that even though this appeared to be a marriage of convenience, it was you Alex chose to be his wife.'

'Yes, but my father——'

'Ha! You don't marry someone just to please a friend!' Stella shook her head, incredulous. 'This is a further demonstration of how little you know your husband. Since he was nineteen years old he's been running that plantation. He's doubled the size of it. He's gone from strength to strength entirely off his own bat. He's got the reins of his life very firmly in his hands. Nobody influences Alex when it comes to running his life. Not me, not Harry—*nobody*! True, he was looking for a wife—but, darling, he's had dozens of girl-friends, all of whom were available. And it was *you* he chose. Now, that has to mean something, doesn't it? It means at least that Alex regards you as very special!'

Gina thought about that for a long moment. Of course Stella was right! And of course—well, a man in his position, a man with his looks and wealth—Alex must have had dozens of girl-friends!

She shot to her feet. 'Stella, may I use your bathroom? I want to repair my make-up.'

'You'd better—you look awful!'

'Oh, Stella . . .' She turned, hugging her stepmother without shyness, kissing her briefly on the cheek. 'I don't know how to thank you. There is hope . . .'

Stella chuckled. 'Darling, the fact that we're friends is thanks enough. If only I'd been able . . . well, I always wanted a daughter, someone just like you. Do you realise I'm old enough to be your mother? And you——' She paused, as if unsure whether she ought to voice her next words. 'You've never had a mother, a woman with whom you could . . . Well, I've been married three times, and if anyone's qualified to give advice on these matters, it's me!'

Gina held on to her hand, in no hurry to cut the interview short. She felt as if a great weight had been lifted from her shoulders. And it felt good. 'I—I hope I see a lot more of you now. I mean, I—I hope I *see* you—that I'm not just writing to you from the other side of the world.'

'Go and fix your face,' said Stella, having difficulty in holding back her own tears.

CHAPTER TEN

'I HOPE you didn't upset Stella.' Alex put down his drink, eyeing her coldly from the other side of the coffee table.

It was a remark which once would have irritated her, but not now. Gina understood Alex's feelings towards Stella—but she was no closer to understanding him. They had been sitting in the lounge of the bungalow for almost half an hour, discussing the business of the copper mine. Alex had neither apologised nor taken the trouble to give his side of the story.

This was proving every bit as difficult as Gina had expected it to be. There were moments when she thought it hopeless, that the gulf between herself and Alex could never be bridged. It was almost like talking to a computer. He was emotionless, cold, as he'd been ever since he had returned from Mombasa. Gina was nervous, scared, but determined to talk with him. She was fighting for her marriage—her life! The resolve she had made as she had patched up her make-up in Stella's bathroom a little over an hour ago would not be shaken. Her stepmother's words were still ringing in her ears, still serving as a lifeline. Alex had married *her*—and that had to stand for something . . .

'Of course I didn't upset Stella. She—she was cross because you hadn't explained it to me.'

'If you're after an apology, you have one. Right? I'm sorry I didn't tell you what was going on. Now you know. And don't you go blabbing to your father!'

Gina was aghast. Just what did he think she was? Totally thoughtless and insensitive? 'Is that why you didn't tell me before? Because you thought I'd let Daddy know?'

There was just the slightest hesitation before he spoke.

'Not exactly. I'd planned on telling you later—after it was properly sorted out. I thought you had enough to cope with for the time being. You had a lot on your mind.'

'You mean our marriage?'

'No,' he scoffed, 'I mean more important things—like your disappointment because your father couldn't finance your business.'

Gina fiddled nervously with the choker around her neck. It was hard to formulate an answer to that. 'Alex, don't you see that when you lied to me about that phone call on our wedding night, it . . . it gave me all sorts of doubts? It didn't exactly help us get off to a good start.'

'So, I lied.' He dismissed her statement with a shrug. Then, as if he began to see the implications, 'Are you telling me that if I hadn't lied to you, everything would be dandy between us? Come off it, Gina. Besides, you've been lying to me for the past month.'

She drew in a sharp breath. 'What do you mean?'

'I mean you've been living a lie every day for the past month. You never tell me what's going through your mind, but you're not as secretive as you think you are. In two quite different ways, you've been living a lie. Firstly, you want me physically just as much as I want you. Secondly, you don't want to be married to me. If we combine the two, it becomes a little complex. But I've figured it out for myself. You're using sex as some sort of weapon, deliberately withholding from me as a way of getting back at me for pushing you into this marriage.'

'No! Alex, no, you're so wrong!' Panic rose within her, but how could she blame him for reaching those conclusions? 'On our wedding night, the phone call, I——' Oh, God, how could she tell him of her real suspicions about his relationship with Stella? He'd be disgusted! 'I—I was nervous that night. That's normal enough, isn't it?'

'Certainly. And I took that into account, didn't I?' He threw the point back at her, his eyes, his voice accusing. It was as if he didn't want to have this conversation, as if he just couldn't be bothered. 'I tried everything; patience, understanding—the lot! But you don't tell me what you're thinking. You don't even talk to me about anything more important than the weather . . .

'And when I think back, I realise you started withdrawing from me the moment we stepped out of the register office. How many brides go to bed on their wedding afternoon? Alone! So don't give me all that rubbish about a phone call that didn't take place until midnight!'

There was anger in his voice now. But at least it was something, some sort of emotion. Alex got to his feet, flinging his jacket on the sofa as he picked up his drink. 'It's three o'clock in the morning. So, if you've quite finished, I think I'll turn in.'

'I haven't finished!' Gina's courage surprised her. Alex stopped in his tracks and turned, looking at her doubtfully. 'I—I'm trying to communicate with you now, Alex. Please—please meet me halfway!'

'Why, certainly.' He smiled. 'How nice it will be to have a real conversation with my wife. One that isn't composed of platitudes.' He was like the man she had met at the airport then, sarcastic, arrogant, seeking to put her down. But she wasn't going to be put down. The only trouble was that she didn't know what to say next—which left her with no choice but the truth.

Alex was looking at her expectantly, unsmiling. There was a muscle twitching in his jaw. 'Well?'

'I w-was hoping we could start again . . .'

'Start again?' He looked at her sardonically. 'Explain yourself.'

Explain herself? What else was there to say? Not only was he not meeting her halfway, he was deliberately making it harder for her!

Gina clenched her fists, her nails digging into the palms of her hands as she forced her eyes to meet with his. 'I-don't-want-the-annulment.'

The silence screamed in her ears. Alex said nothing.

His facial expression didn't change one iota. 'Alex, I want to stay married to you.'

'Indeed? And why is that?'

Why? Damn him, he wasn't going to strip her of all her pride! She wasn't going to wear her heart on her sleeve! 'Because—because I think we could make a success of it.'

'I see.' His tone was dull, flat.

Gina cringed inwardly, waiting for the sarcasm—waiting for his answer. Oh, but he'd reverted to type! How could he do this? How could he make her bare her soul, then leave her squirming, wriggling helplessly like a worm on a hook!

'I don't think it's a good idea, Gina. I don't like the ground rules.'

She shot to her feet, too angry to be upset. The little pride she had retained, and all her composure, was shot to pieces. 'Damn you to hell, Alex Craig! Did you marry me only to get access to my body?'

The look on his face terrified her then. 'You bitch!' He crossed the room in two strides.

'Let me go!' she screamed as his mouth came down on hers, his hands holding her arms behind her back, leaving her helpless, vulnerable—available! Her mind spun as she realised what was happening. But she felt no fear—just a raging, searing anger. 'You're obsessed!' she shrieked. 'Why didn't you marry Mandy Miller, if sex is all you're after?'

'Why, you little fool, I wouldn't have married her if she'd been the last woman on earth!' With one hand he held her arms in place, his free hand reaching up to tear the dress from her shoulders.

Gina fought frantically against him as his lips moved over her face, her neck. His words barely registered; she could think of nothing but what he was doing, nothing but her hatred of him. Her naked breasts were straining against his chest, her struggles serving only to excite him further. 'I hate you, Alex Craig. I hate you!'

But he just laughed at her, his hand coming round to

cup her breast, his fingers pulling tauntingly against the nipple. 'It's no good, Gina,' he grated. 'I'm going to take you now if I've got to force you! I'm going to show you what you've been missing all this time. And then you'll know what it's like to be obsessed!' And with that, he scooped her up bodily, throwing her over his shoulder as he had done once before—a hundred years ago.

Her fists were pounding against his back, her legs kicking about wildly. Still he laughed as he carried her into his bedroom, his arm across her back, holding her in place like a vice.

She was falling, screaming, fighting—sprawled out on the bed with only one second's freedom before Alex moved his body over hers. Her screams were cut off in mid-air as his lips came down on hers, bruising, demanding, punishing ... until suddenly everything stood still. Time, thoughts, emotions, everything stopped but the passion that was consuming her now, that electricity, that magnetism which had once held her prisoner. Now they were both imprisoned by it.

Alex's lips moved to her neck, her breasts, his entire attitude changing as he sought no longer to punish but to carry her with him to that point, that pitch of ecstasy she had not yet experienced. His hands moved down over her stomach, and on and on. As his fingers sought out that most intimate part of her, Gina's body arched against him and a moan of pure desire tore from her throat.

Gina had forgotten what it was like to sleep so soundly. The waking up process was rather like surfacing from a tunnel, a dark, warm and comforting place. She didn't stir. She just lay, quietly, watching the narrow strips of light from the shutters, playing on the bedroom floor.

She had also forgotten what it was like to wake up and look forward to the day ahead of her. But last night had been the turning point, hadn't it? Surely—surely everything would be all right now?

She smiled as Alex stirred beside her, his arm a comforting, comfortable weight on her hip. She snuggled closer to him, turning slightly so she could watch his face in sleep.

But Alex was awake, smiling sleepily. 'Good morning, darling. How are you feeling?'

The endearment registered immediately and with it came a sudden rush of confidence. She tilted her face up to his, unaware that the look on her face told him everything he needed to know. 'Obsessed,' she smiled. 'Possessed!'

'Possessed, eh?' His grin was wicked, the deep blue eyes sparkling with laughter. 'Then you'd better go and make me some coffee.'

'Oh, no!' She stuck her tongue out. 'Maybe I'm possessed, but I'm not your slave. You can make your own coffee. And bring me some tea while you're at it.'

'I see you're as cheeky as ever.' He started tickling her, his fingers dancing around her ribs until she was giggling like a schoolgirl. 'You are my slave, woman. You will do my bidding!' He planted a kiss on her nose, moving his body over hers as he continued to tickle, holding her in place, helpless with laughter.

When his arms locked around her back and his mouth came down on hers she responded instantly, knowing, now, the delights which were in store for her, realising that her husband's lovemaking was something she could not live without. And yes, in this respect at least she was his slave.

It was much, much later when Gina finally glanced at Alex's watch on the bedside table. 'Help!' She pulled away from the circle of his arms, slipping into the black shirt he had worn the night before. 'Alex, it's almost noon!'

'I know. It's very time-consuming, being married to a sex maniac.'

She threw up her hands in despair, dashing to the kitchen in double-quick time. There was no one around, no

Lanu, no Botana. The place was as quiet as a graveyard.

'What's the panic?' Alex came into the kitchen, wrapping a pale blue *kikoy* around his waist.

'Lunch!' Gina spoke over her shoulder as she hastily filled the kettle. 'You were going to ask my parents over to lunch! What time did you tell them?'

'Ah, you can relax. They're coming to dinner instead. Stella said that would be more convenient for them. She'll be spending the morning clearing up after the party.'

'I see. And where are Lanu and Botana?'

'They're over at Stella's, helping her to clean up.'

Gina was fiddling with cups and saucers, keeping her back to him so he wouldn't see her nervousness. It was different now, standing in the kitchen in the cold light of day, different from being in bed with him where the distractions prohibited any kind of normal conversation.

She turned to face him then. It would be much easier to clear the air straight away, to find out whether ... 'Alex, will you—will you be seeing your lawyer tomorrow?'

It seemed an age before he answered. His eyes were locked with hers, probing, seeking. 'No. I intend to stay here until Wednesday or Thursday. In between visits with your parents, I'm going to tie you to the bed and make mad passionate love to you for the next four days. What do you think of that idea?'

It wasn't much. It was by no means all she wanted to hear, but it was all she had. She clung to it like a lifeline, praying that this was his way of telling her she was, indeed, very special. Or was he committing himself to nothing more than a four-day honeymoon? Only time would tell. Of one thing she could be certain; their marriage, she herself, was very much on trial. She would have to face each day as it came.

Alex said nothing more. He was waiting for her answer, and she smiled over at him, trying hard to mask all her doubts and fears. 'I'll find you some rope.'

CHAPTER ELEVEN

'ALICE DENBY? Of course I remember you! We met at the Smithsons' barbecue two weeks ago ... Yes ... We're fine, thanks.' Gina sat down in the chair beside the telephone. Her hands were covered with flour. She had been in the midst of teaching the cook how to make simple short-crust pastry when the telephone interrupted her. It seemed like an odd sort of activity, but while their Indian cook was an absolute wizard at conjuring up exotic dishes, he had yet to learn the basics.

'Yes, Mrs Denby—Alice—that would be lovely. But I'd better check with Alex. Can you hold on for a moment ... I'll be right back.'

Gina left the receiver dangling on its wire and dashed into the study, only to find that Alex was on the phone, too. She signalled to him and he held his hand over the receiver.

'I've got Alice Denby on the other line. She wants to know if we'd like to go to a dinner party at her house on Thursday.'

'It's fine by me,' Alex smiled. 'If you'd like to go, Gina.'

He always said that, always left the ball in her court as far as socialising was concerned. They were frequently asked out, but they didn't frequently go out. In fact the last time they had gone socialising was just over two weeks ago, when they had returned from Malindi. They had gone to the barbecue where Gina had met Alice and Peter Denby for the first time, and she had liked them both instantly.

'Well, I think it's nice of her to ask us,' she told Alex. 'I'll accept the invitation.'

Alex nodded, getting back to his own telephone conversation. But just as she was closing the study door, Gina caught his opening sentence—and felt the hair at the back of her neck bristle. 'Sorry about that, Mandy.' Alex's voice had a smile in it. 'What were you saying?'

Mandy Miller! Ringing him on his private line! What for, and, more to the point, how often had she done that during the past two weeks? She had not set foot on the *shamba*, and Gina had begun to think she'd given up on her quest. Evidently she hadn't.

Mandy Miller was still very much a thorn in Gina's side. She still didn't know the truth surrounding Alex's visit to Mombasa. Had he taken Mandy with him? Had he made love to her that on that fateful Sunday, after he had announced his decision regarding the annulment? It was a nauseating thought. It was a thought Gina had pushed into the recesses of her mind.

Only then did it occur to her that she was repeating her mistakes, bottling up important matters which were a source of worry to her. Doing precisely that had almost wrecked her marriage. So she must speak out. She must find out the truth; tackle Alex about it at the earliest opportunity.

If her worst fears were realised, there was nothing she could do about it, of course. It was too late. And it was all her own fault, anyway.

But there was plenty she could do to hedge against future dangers. She didn't think for one minute that Alex would go to bed with Mandy at this stage. Gina's sex life with her husband was the one thing about their marriage which was perfect. In general terms her relationship with him was much better than it had been—but there was still a lot remaining to be said. And she was not so confident of Alex's feelings for her that she could disregard the danger of Mandy Miller's presence in their lives. For some obscure reason, Alex liked Mandy—he had said as much. But in Gina's eyes Mandy was a predator—and a very cunning one at that.

She went back to the kitchen and resumed her pastry-making lesson. But her mind was not on the job in hand, and she spent the entire afternoon rehearsing what she would say to Alex—after she had managed to broach the subject of Mandy in the first place.

She never dreamt that Alex would bring up the subject before she did, but as they were walking into the dining room that evening, he told her about Mandy's call.

'Mandy phoned? Today?' Gina kept her voice light, letting Alex think this was news to her. 'What did she want?'

'Nothing in particular.' He smiled. 'She just wanted to say hello.'

Gina took that with a pinch of salt. If that had been Mandy's real reason for ringing, why not call round instead? As she used to. Why ring Alex on his private line, when the chances were that Gina wouldn't find out about it?

'I take it she was saying hello to both of us?'

'Of course.' Alex filled their wineglasses and tucked into his soup. 'Hey, aren't you hungry?'

'What? Oh, yes!' Gina followed suit a little reluctantly. Her appetite had suddenly vanished. 'I—I've been meaning to ask you about—about what you told Mandy on that Sunday when . . . I mean, did you tell her about the annulment?'

'Good God, Gina,' Alex looked appalled, 'of course not! I wouldn't discuss such private matters with other people—you should know that by now.'

'I do really. I mean . . . well, it was obvious we'd had a row. I just wondered what—what you'd said.'

'I told her we'd had a lovers' tiff, that's all.' He gave her a crooked smile.

Gina managed to smile back at him. Her mouth had gone dry and she couldn't taste the soup she was eating. 'You—you drove off somewhere. Alex, where did you go?'

'To the shooting club. Ah, Kimau . . .' As the old man approached with a tray of food, Alex's eyes lit up. 'What have you got there?'

Kimau treated Gina to his broadest smile. He answered his master in his own language. Didn't he know how to describe steak and kidney pie in English? Maybe he'd never seen one before . . .

'I don't believe it!' Alex's deep, rumbling laughter might have been infectious if Gina were not so tense. 'Darling, how did you do it? How did you get Ali to make a simple dish like this?'

'It was not easy, bwana,' Kimau answered for her. 'Memsab had to do a lot of talking. And Ali has confided in me that he thinks you are both—er——' he broke off, looking for the right word and not finding it, 'both very strange if you can eat this sort of food. He thinks it will not be good for you!'

'I'll be the judge of that!' Alex told him. He was still smiling as Kimau left the room. 'Dish up, then, you clever girl. And don't be sparing. Do you know, I haven't had steak and kidney pie for years! Not since my mother was alive.'

At any other time Gina would have encouraged him to go on, to talk about his family, his past. But not now. She had other things on her mind. 'You were saying—you went to the shooting club. What club is that?'

'I thought Mandy had mentioned it to you. Gina, you can take that frown off your face, we don't go shooting animals! It's clay-pigeon shooting!'

Gina was not a bit concerned about what they shot at. The only target she was interested in was the one Mandy Miller had her sights on. She was feeling better already, though. Mandy had mentioned something about a monthly shoot, and it was perfectly feasible that Alex had gone there. Perhaps as a means of giving vent to his anger . . .

'I've been a member for fifteen years,' Alex was saying

now, 'but Mandy only joined a few months ago, after she came back to live with her parents.'

There was only one more thing she needed to know. And if Alex's answer held water, she could accept that he had made his trip to Mombasa alone.

'You got back very late that night. What did you do after you'd left the club?'

'I went back to her place——' He looked up sharply, as if he didn't quite understand what she was getting at. 'I went back to her place and sat drinking and chatting with her father till the early hours of the morning. What is this, Gina, why am I getting the third degree?'

Gina looked down at her plate. She'd had good reason to be suspicious—very good reason! So how come he was making her feel guilty? To hell with it, she must finish this conversation regardless. It was all part of communication, all part of what she'd yet to achieve with her husband.

'Alex, I don't like Mandy Miller.'

'So what's new?' he said levelly.

'You once said—you once said you wouldn't have married her if she'd been the last woman on earth.'

'That's right. And I meant it.' There was an edge to his voice now, as if he didn't care for the way the conversation was going. 'I wouldn't entertain the idea of marrying someone who spends half her day in the beauty parlour, a woman who's so used to being waited on that she can't fasten her own shoes. But let's get to the crux of the matter. What you really want to know is whether I went to bed with Mandy—a month ago, or five years ago. The answer is no. I've never taken her to bed.'

Gina put down her knife and fork. 'Alex, please, don't get angry with me. It isn't you I don't trust—honestly. It's her! Darling, she's not a fool. She knew there was something wrong with our marriage. And she's still phoning you—on your private line. Don't you see——'

Alex held up his hands in a gesture of disbelief. 'I'm not angry with you. Look again. Look at me, Gina. See? I'm not angry, I'm not even annoyed—but I am disturbed because it's taken you two weeks to bring this thing out in the open. You've had your doubts about me and Mandy all this time. Haven't you?'

Gina nodded, embarrassed. She could see what was coming—and she'd left herself wide open for it.

'Until tonight, I had no idea.' He sighed. 'Again, I had no idea what was going through your mind. Why didn't you ask me before? I don't mind answering your questions—provided I know the reason behind them. Darling, how can I possibly put your mind at rest when I don't know what I'm being accused of?'

There was no answer to that. He was absolutely right, of course. 'I—I'm sorry. I'm trying to change my ways—honestly I am. I—I did bring it out in the open tonight . . .'

'Because I told you that Mandy phoned,' he stated. 'Keep trying. Keep talking. Let's clear this up once and for all.'

'There's no more to say.' Gina shrugged, believing she was telling the truth. 'You've answered my questions. So now I know.'

'Very well,' he said patiently, 'then I'll do the talking. You brought up the subject of Mandy tonight because knowing she'd phoned me made you feel threatened. I'm perfectly well aware that Mandy had designs on me. Certainly she knew that something was wrong between us—anyone with eyes could see that much. As you say, she's not a fool. She knew that if there was any chance of—er—getting to me, it was on that particular Sunday, when we'd had the row. She knew we'd fought over something serious, despite the fact that I tried to play it down.'

He reached for her hand, but Gina kept quite still. She was at a loss to understand him. How could he be aware that Mandy had designs on him and not tell her where to get off? He was *married* now, for heaven's sake! Was Gina supposed to put up with Mandy Miller draping herself all over the place, making surreptitious phone calls, for the next thirty years?

'Say it aloud, Gina. For goodness' sake, trust me for once.'

She reached for his hand then. 'Oh, Alex, I do trust you. But I don't understand you.' She told him every thought that had gone through her mind.

'You don't know it was a surreptitious call. How do you know she hadn't tried the other number? The line was engaged. You were talking to Alice Denby when Mandy's call came through to the study.'

Gina didn't answer that one. There was no denying she had a suspicious mind. 'But I—I just don't see how you can like her. She's always posing and flirting——'

'Look, Gina, I've known Mandy Miller since she was six years old, that's when her parents first moved out here. She was a pretty little girl, and she learned the flirting game at a very early age. It's just the way she is. But at least she's honest. She's after a husband, and virtually anyone will do—provided he's rich. You see, I know her better than you think.'

'And you treat as you find, don't you?'

'That's right. And I find her pleasant enough. She's just—just another person. The girl who lives next door! She's been helpful to me in the past, so I'm not going to tell her to keep away, if that's what you're angling for.'

That was, in fact, precisely what Gina wanted him to do. But Alex was too kind to do such a thing without good reason—and Mandy Miller didn't bother him one way or the other.

She bothered Gina, however. 'Well, I find her unpleasant. She annoys me. I feel inclined to chase her off these premises with a shotgun the next time she turns up.'

Alex was not amused. 'That's your prerogative.' He shook his head, as if Gina had disappointed him in some way. 'Just let me make one thing clear: Mandy Miller is not in any way a threat, to you—to us. She never has been and she never will be.'

Gina felt tons better. It had been a worthwhile conversation if only because he had helped her to speak her mind. And it hadn't been so difficult, after all. Alex had given her the reassurance she needed.

The conversation went zipping through Gina's mind once more when she and Alex arrived at the Denbys' house on the following Thursday evening. She used the memory of Alex's reassurance to help her keep a civil tongue when she suddenly found herself face to face with Mandy Miller. If she had known Mandy was going to be there, Gina would have refused the invitation. But it was too late now.

Alice and Peter Denby were kindly, charming people who seemed to spend most of their lives giving and attending parties. They seemed to know everyone—and everyone's business. They greeted Alex and Gina like long-lost friends and made all their guests feel very much at home. There were fourteen people for dinner, including the host and hostess, and Mandy was the last to arrive.

She made her grand entrance into the Denbys' living room wearing a low-cut emerald green dress which made all heads turn in her direction, even though the colour didn't suit her very much. She waved gaily to the room at large—and made a beeline for Alex and Gina, who were standing in a corner talking to a middle-aged South African they had just been introduced to.

'Robert Wallis—meet Mandy. Mandy Miller.' Alex made the introductions and Gina watched the long-legged blonde go into her posing routine. The South African seemed to have difficulty in keeping his eyes off Mandy's cleavage and while Mandy eagerly lapped up the admiration, it was Gina she turned her attention to at the first opportunity.

'You and Alex seem to be getting on remarkably well these days.' Mandy's eyes flitted towards the men, who had quickly become engrossed in their own conversation, before settling on Gina's face.

Gina's fingers tightened on the glass she was holding, but she gave no outward sign of her irritation. 'You find it remarkable? I should have thought it perfectly natural.'

'Oh, come off it, Gina.' Mandy kept her voice low, that false smile pulling at her lips. 'The last time I saw you, you looked as if you were on the brink of divorce or something.'

Gina's laugh was a tinkle, but it sounded hollow even to her own ears. 'That's a little dramatic.'

'It happens,' Mandy said dryly. 'And let's face it, you hardly got off to a good start. I'll give you six months before you end up in the divorce courts. You mark my words.'

Gina had to bite back her retort. Alex's reassurance was all very well, but Mandy Miller was doing her level best to interfere with their marriage, to undermine Gina's confidence. For once in her life Gina was stuck for words. At least, she couldn't think of a moderate reply—one that wouldn't set off a full-scale row. With a satisfied smirk, Mandy turned her attention back to the men. Happily, it was only a few minutes later that Alice Denby announced that dinner was about to be served.

The evening turned out to be an awful strain. Alice had seated everyone boy, girl, boy, girl. On Gina's left was her husband and on her right, at the head of the table, was a rather flushed Peter Denby who had clearly had too much to drink before the food was served. Halfway through the first course he leaned towards Gina, speaking in tones of confidentiality.

'That chap across the table, Bob Wallis—he's Alice's cousin. She put him next to Mandy in the hope that they might hit it off together. He's a bachelor.'

Gina gave him her wide-eyed look. 'I see. I'm afraid it isn't working. Mandy's directing most of her chatter towards my husband.'

'Oh, my dear, you mustn't let that bother you. We all know she's got a soft spot for Alex. But she flirts with everyone! You have to feel sorry for her, really. She thinks she's got something to prove . . .'

Gina looked at him curiously. Physically, he was not unlike her father, but that was as far as the resemblance went. Peter Denby was a gossip, but there was nothing malicious about him, and Gina couldn't help liking him.

'. . . I mean, it must have been a blow to her confidence.'

She smiled. 'That Alex married me, you mean?'

'Eh? No! I mean her husband walking out on her when they'd only been married six months. Didn't you know? Yes, six months—and he left her for another woman.' He glanced over at Mandy and shook his head. 'You wouldn't credit that, would you?'

'No,' said Gina, incredulous, 'you wouldn't credit that, Peter.' Without thinking, her eyes travelled over to Mandy, narrowing shrewdly as she absorbed what she had just been told.

The showdown came the following morning. Gina knew it would happen sooner or later, even if her husband didn't. She was far too high-spirited to allow anyone to get away with prolonged sarcasm. Besides, Mandy Miller was insulting her intelligence. Did she think for one minute that Gina didn't realise what she was up to?

It was a working day, a Friday. Alex and Gina had overslept as a result of the previous evening's dinner party, from which it had been very difficult to get away. Gina's head was a little fuzzy when she woke up. It was Kimau's day off, and they had neglected to tell one of the housemen to wake them at their usual time. It was nine o'clock when she slipped quietly out of bed, leaving Alex to sleep until she brought him some coffee.

Jacob was waiting for her when she went downstairs. He was sitting on the kitchen doorstep, whining.

Gina tied a knot in the belt of her towelling housecoat and let him in. 'What's all this? You got fed here yesterday, and the day before. This is becoming a habit, Jacob. Your other benefactors will wonder what they've done to offend you!'

Jacob cooked his head to one side, big brown eyes looking up at her curiously. He trotted after her as she filled the kettle. 'All right, all right. Human beings first, Jacob. I've just got to have a cup of tea! I'll feed you afterwards.'

But Jacob didn't care for that idea. He set off whining again so Gina fed him while the tea was brewing. She was just in the midst of pouring herself a cup when she sensed that someone was watching her. And it wasn't the dog.

'Well, well, isn't this a nice little domestic scene?'

Gina's hand jerked. She had just become aware of someone's presence when Mandy Miller's voice reached her ears. She wasn't angry; she knew precisely how she was going to handle this encounter. She was merely startled at the way Mandy had crept up on her.

'Good morning, Mandy. Would you like a cup of tea? I've just made some.' Gina smiled to herself at the sight of Mandy lounging against the door-jamb, wearing too much make-up and too few clothes, as usual.

'You must be joking! I haven't drunk tea since I was ten years old.'

'Well, it's a little early for alcohol. And the coffee hasn't perked yet, I've only just put it on. Needless to say, we don't keep instant coffee in this household.'

'Needless to say. Where's Alex?'

'In bed. Asleep.' Gina sat down at the kitchen table, motioning her forward. But Mandy was quite content to stay where she was.

'There was something I meant to ask him last night—a

favour. So you won't mind if I hang around till he comes down, will you?'

'Not at all.' Gina kept her composure beautifully as Mandy's eyes travelled over her face, devoid of make-up, and her dressing gown which was knee-length, white, and spoke of nothing but practicality.

'It looks as if the honeymoon's over,' Mandy smirked. 'According to the rules, you two should still be lying in bed together till noon. After all, Alex doesn't need to work—if there's something more interesting to keep him at home. But then it doesn't take long for the glitter to wear off, does it? No doubt you've discovered by now that marriages aren't made in heaven. Especially yours, which was a rushed job, to say the least. It crossed my mind that you were pregnant, although come to think of it, there wasn't time even for that.'

There was a long, long silence. Mandy was smiling as if she had spent the past minute and a half talking about the weather. As for Gina, something strange was happening to her. For the first time ever she was seeing Mandy Miller for what she really was—pathetic, frustrated and very, very bitter.

It would have been so easy for Gina to beat her at her own game, to better her snide remarks, but she resisted it, and to her own surprise she suddenly discovered it was not difficult to resist. Mandy Miller was green with envy, racked with jealousy because Gina had achieved in such a short time that which Mandy had been angling for for months.

Little did Mandy know that she would never have landed Alex Craig if she had worked at it till Doomsday. But Gina knew it, and with that there came a tremendous sense of superiority. Gina had Alex. Mandy had no one. Gina had nothing to be jealous of, nothing to envy Mandy Miller for. It was then, in the space of a few seconds, that she realised fully the truth of Alex's words: Mandy Miller was not a threat.

Seeing her through different eyes made Gina realise how very easy it would be to handle her, to get rid of her. She didn't need a shotgun; all that was needed was a little plain speaking, a little straight talk.

With an expression which was impassive and a voice which was genuinely devoid of emotion, Gina let her have it. 'No, unfortunately I'm not pregnant. Not yet. You were wrong about that. You're wrong about the honeymoon, too. It hasn't even begun. As a matter of fact, Alex and I are leaving for our official honeymoon at the end of next week.'

Gina refilled her teacup as she spoke calmly and precisely, without hesitation, leaving no room for Mandy to get a word in. 'Now, you might say the honeymoon has been delayed a little. But all marriages have their teething troubles. All relationships have their teething troubles. Take you and me, for instance. We didn't get off to a good start, did we? But I hope that's all over with now, Mandy. I think it was really nice of you to phone the other day and say hello. After all, you and Alex are old friends, and I want you to know that we'll both welcome you to our home any time you care to call.'

Mandy Miller recoiled visibly. She was shocked to the core, at a total loss to understand the change in Gina's attitude. Suspicion, puzzlement and disbelief flitted across her face.

But Gina hadn't finished yet. 'There's one thing you must bear in mind, however. Your prediction about my marriage is something else you've got wrong. Alex will not leave me after six months—for you, or for any other woman. I shall still be married to him when you're a very, very old lady. You see, I love him more than life itself, and he's deeply in love with me. Is that plain enough? And if you don't believe it, you can ask him yourself. So you may visit us as a neighbour, as an old friend of Alex—but you'll be wasting your time. There's nothing for you here, and I'm well aware of what you're trying——'

Mandy Miller had gone. She turned and bolted with her nose held high in the air and her face a tight mask set in mahogany skin.

Gina didn't move. She went right on drinking her tea. The kitchen was as quiet then as it had been before the intrusion, the only sound coming from Jacob as he lapped up his water. Now, he was the only audience Gina had—or so she thought.

'Well done!'

At the sound of her husband's voice, Gina's heart started pounding frantically. 'Alex! You——' She put down her cup with hands that were trembling. 'You—you heard? I—how much did you hear?'

He was standing in the doorway leading to the hall, barefooted, bare-chested, wearing just a pair of navy-blue slacks, his golden hair still ruffled from sleep. 'All of it.'

'All of it? You were eavesdropping . . .'

'Certainly.' He smiled as he walked towards her, taking hold of her hand and pulling her to her feet. 'So you've finally staked your claim!' His arms went about her waist and he hugged her very, very gently—as if she were made of glass. 'You handled her beautifully, Gina. You see, all you had to do was speak your mind. I couldn't do it for you.'

'Yes, I see that now—finally! I—I should've done it weeks ago.' Relief flooded over her, not only because he approved of what she had done but also because it seemed that she had not been too presumptuous in all that she had told Mandy Miller. Alex did love her—he had to! He couldn't possibly have been so patient, have put up with her continued stupidity unless he loved her.

'But what was all that about a honeymoon? You might have told me if you'd made some arrangements!'

He was laughing at her, teasing her. 'Oh, well, I—er—I just used that to help me make a point. It was just . . . just a little white lie.'

'I see! Well, we can't make a liar out of you, can we? So we will go away next week—for a month or two. Darling, I'm very proud of you. It's painful, isn't it, the growing-up process?'

Gina looked up at him, only to see there was no laughter in his eyes. 'Oh, Alex, is that what you've been waiting for? For me to grow up?'

He held her tightly then, possessively. 'In some ways, yes. What about the other things you said to Mandy? Were you just saying those to help you make a point?'

'Don't you know?' She pulled away from him, wanting to look directly into his eyes as she told him, for the first time, that she loved him. 'Don't you know that I love you? Yes, I meant it. I love you more than life itself.'

'It's nice to hear you say it.' He smiled ruefully. 'It's rather ironical you should say it to Mandy Miller before you said it to me, don't you think?'

Gina rested her head against his chest, trembling inwardly and having difficulty in getting her next words past the constriction in her throat. 'I'm sorry, Alex. I— I've been so stupid, so often. I don't know why you married me. I can't imagine what you ever saw in me. I was so horrible——'

With a kiss, he cut off her words, his lips brushing lightly, briefly against her own. 'I married you because I loved you. Oh, the girl I took home from the airport had all the characteristics I was definitely not looking for in a wife! I didn't fall *in love* with you—it was far more subtle than that. But damn it all, in spite of myself I grew to love you as I got to know you. You were so young, so spirited—and so vulnerable and afraid. In other words, when I looked behind your disguise, I saw a girl who needed very much to be loved, and something in me responded to that.'

He moved away from her slightly, holding her at arm's length and watching her carefully, as if he were unsure how she would react. 'I couldn't *tell* you, Gina. Do you see that? I was afraid you'd resent it. Every time I tried to talk about your real personality, you pulled the tough-guy act on me. The way you were in those days, I didn't dare tell you you needed protecting, loving, security, stability . . . all the things which had been missing from your life. I couldn't risk frightening you off, and your pride would have prevented you accepting it. I waited, and I've continued to wait, for you to learn these things about yourself.

'Harry also knew what you needed. He's aware of his shortcomings as far as your upbringing is concerned. Darling, he wasn't trying to get rid of you in suggesting marriage to me. He knew I was right for you. It's just that he doesn't know the meaning of the word tact. Patience is not one of his——'

Gina put a finger over his lips, her heart bursting with love because he was taking the trouble to excuse Harry, not knowing that she'd long ago forgiven her father for his heavy-handed attitude. 'It's all right, darling. Getting to know my father—and Stella—has been part of the growing process. I understand him now better than ever before. I underestimated his farsightedness. Let's face it, he didn't do any harm, even if he did behave like a—a——'

'Bulldozer?' Alex threw back his head and laughed. 'I wasn't going to complain! As far as I was concerned, he was giving you a shove in the right direction!'

Gina was laughing, too. Then, unpredictably, suddenly she was crying. 'Nobody pushed me into this marriage! I wanted to marry you. I was in love with you! It happened the other way round with me, Alex. I—I fell in love with you first. And then I loved you more and more as time went on. I——' She broke off, sniffing as Alex reached into his pocket and pulled out a big white hanky. 'Wh-when you said you wanted an annulment, it almost destroyed me!'

'Ssh, don't cry. Sit down.' He eased her on to a kitchen

chair. 'I'll get us some coffee, then I'll explain my reasons for that business about the annulment.'

She did as he bade her, fitful little sobs making her tremble as she thought about how very close they had been to disaster.

'I had to force things to a head, Gina. I couldn't live like that, loving you, wanting you. You gave me no hint of your feelings, you avoided my attempts to communicate, withdrew from me in every sense of the word. I understand it better now, of course, but do you see how it looked to me? I'm not a mind-reader. There was only one conclusion I could reach—here, drink this.'

He pushed a steaming mug of coffee towards her, adding milk and sugar for her, and she sipped it slowly, her tears gradually subsiding.

'I concluded that I'd been wrong in my assessment of you. I thought you must have really meant all that you'd once said about marriage—about it being an institution, too, in the sense of it holding one prisoner. I thought you were punishing me for talking you into it, for getting that ring on your finger when you were at your weakest point.

'But I'd deliberately given you an escape clause, even as I persuaded you to marry me. I told you it wasn't irreversible. I did that because I had my doubts as to how you'd adjust. I was afraid to tell you how much I needed you, wanted you. I didn't want you feeling *obliged* to stay with me. Telling you I wanted us to split was the last resort of a desperate man, the ultimate test. Something had to give, Gina. I wasn't going to allow you to put me through hell any longer——'

She stared at him, horrified. 'I wasn't—I mean, I didn't want——'

'I know that now. I'm trying to explain how it looked from my point of view. So I said I wanted the annulment. My trip to Mombasa was deliberate, too. I wanted to give you a few days alone in order to make up your mind. My God, you left it until the last minute——'

'Stop! Please, Alex! This is so upsetting. To think that we've both . . . darling, let's go to bed. Make love to me. Now!'

'No.' He said it firmly, unsmiling. To soften the blow, he reached for her hand. 'This is a very important conversation we're having. You've got to understand that the first time I realised you loved me was when you told me you wanted to stay married. It was only then that I knew something weird had gone on in your mind . . . Gina, will you stop looking at me with those big beautiful eyes. I'm immune!'

She laughed outrageously, pulling her chair closer to his.

'I knew we had a great deal to sort out, that it would take time. You know, I could have killed you when you accused me of just wanting your body . . . Now, I see that the reverse applies! Gina, will you take your hands off my chest—stop nuzzling me, you wanton!' He got to his feet, moving his chair well away from her.

'What was I saying? Ah, yes, I knew our problems weren't over . . . Gina, what are you doing? Put that dressing gown back on! How can you expect me to make love to you when I'm only just getting to know you?'

Gina chuckled, inching her way towards him with outstretched arms. 'I'm the modern type. Make love first—make acquaintance later!'

'You're a wicked woman, Gina Craig. Wicked, cheeky, unpredictable, disobedient, stubborn—will you *stop* that!' His face broke out into a smile; that familiar, lazy, insolent smile which never failed to send shivers down her spine.

'Oh, to hell with it,' he said, 'we'll talk later!'

Harlequin® Plus

LUDWIG VAN BEETHOVEN

Gina and Alex believe they have little in common—until they listen to the famous *Moonlight Sonata* and discover their mutual love for the music of Beethoven. Ludwig van Beethoven was the most influential composer of his time, and many regard him as the greatest composer of the nineteenth century.

Born in Bonn, Germany, in 1770, Beethoven belonged to a family with a strong musical tradition—his father and grandfather had both sung in a cathedral choir. Ludwig demonstrated his musical talents very early, and when he was seventeen he was sent to study with the famous Austrian composer Wolfgang Mozart. However, his studies were cut short by the death of his mother and he returned to Bonn, where for several years he wrote music on commission. He frequently even ghostwrote pieces for local aristocrats who wanted to pretend that they were composers!

Eventually Beethoven left for Vienna—at that time the cultural center of Europe. He achieved great success there, composing many of his most famous works. Tragically, at the pinnacle of his career, Beethoven became totally deaf. Weary and depressed that he could no longer perform on his beloved piano, he contemplated suicide. However, his friends rallied around, and he soon recovered from his despondency. In fact, he wrote some of his best pieces at this time, even though he would never hear them performed.

In 1827 Beethoven contracted pneumonia and died. His funeral was attended by approximately twenty thousand people. And music lovers all over the world mourned the passing of one of the greatest composers of the era.

HELP HARLEQUIN PICK
1982's GREATEST ROMANCE!

We're taking a poll to find the most romantic couple (real, not fictional) of 1982. Vote for any one you like, but please vote and mail in your ballot today. As Harlequin readers, you're the real romance experts!

Here's a list of suggestions to get you started. Circle your choice, **or** print the names of the couple you think is the most romantic in the space below.

Prince of Wales/Princess of Wales

Luke/Laura (General Hospital stars)

Gilda Radner/Gene Wilder

Jacqueline Bisset/Alexander Godunov

Mark Harmon/Christina Raines

Carly Simon/Al Corley

Susan Seaforth/Bill Hayes

Burt Bacharach/Carole Bayer Sager

_____

(please print)

_____

_____

Please mail to: Maureen Campbell
 Harlequin Books
 225 Duncan Mill Road
 Don Mills, Ontario, Canada
 M3B 3K9

POLL-1

Harlequin Romances

The books that let you escape
into the wonderful world of romance!
Trips to exotic places…interesting
plots…meeting memorable people…
the excitement of love…. These are
integral parts of Harlequin Romances —
the heartwarming novels read by
women everywhere.

Many early issues are now available.
Choose from this great selection!

Choose from this list of Harlequin Romance editions.*

*Some of these book were originally published under different titles.